il

FAUX FINISHED

FAUX FINISHED

PEG MARBERG

WHEELER
CHIVERS

This Large Print edition is published by Wheeler Publishing, Waterville, Maine, USA and by BBC Audiobooks Ltd, Bath, England.
Wheeler Publishing is an imprint of Thomson Gale, a part of The Thomson Corporation.
Wheeler is a trademark and used herein under license.
An Interior Design Mystery.

The text of this Large Print edition is unabridged.
Other aspects of the book may vary from the original edition.
Set in 16 pt. Plantin.

LIBRARY OF CONGRESS CATALOGING-IN-PUBLICATION DATA

Marberg, Peg.
  Faux finished / by Peg Marberg.
    p. cm. — (Wheeler Publishing large print cozy mystery)
  "An Interior Design Mystery."
  ISBN-13: 978-1-59722-542-7 (lg. print : pbk. : alk. paper)
  ISBN-10: 1-59722-542-8 (lg. print : pbk. : alk. paper)
  1. Interior decoration — Fiction. 2. Indiana — Fiction. 3. Large type books. I. Title.
  PS3613.A728F38 2007
  813'.6—dc22   2007011037

BRITISH LIBRARY CATALOGUING-IN-PUBLICATION DATA AVAILABLE

Published in 2007 in the U.S. by arrangement with The Berkley Publishing Group, a member of Penguin Group (USA) Inc.
Published in 2007 in the U.K. by arrangement with The Berkley Publishing Group, a division of Penguin Group (USA) Inc.

U.K. Hardcover: 978 1 405 64184 5 (Chivers Large Print)
U.K. Softcover: 978 1 405 64185 2 (Camden Large Print)

Printed in the United States of America on permanent paper
10 9 8 7 6 5 4 3 2 1

This book is dedicated to my family, and in particular to my grandson, Steve Rzyski. His faith in me, like his own talent for writing, is awesome.

I wish to thank my husband, Ed, whose love, loyalty, and patience sustained me throughout the writing of this book. I also would like to thank my editor, Sandra Harding, for making me a believer in miracles.

CITIZENS OF SEVILLE, INDIANA

Jean Hastings Interior designer and amateur sleuth.

Charlie Hastings Jean's husband and retired investment counselor.

JR Cusak The Hastings's married daughter and Jean's business partner.

Matt Cusak JR's husband and police lieutenant.

Kerry and Kelly Cusak JR and Matt's children.

Mary England Charlie's twin sister and Jean's best friend.

Denny England Mary's husband and owner of England's Fine Furniture.

Rollie Stevens Seville's chief of police.

Doc Parker, M.D. General practitioner

Vernon Higgins Owner of Valley Labs, a pharmaceutical conglomerate.

Vanessa Higgins Vernon's wife and president of the Sleepy Hollow Country Club's board of directors.

Harrison Fowler Manager of the Sleepy Hollow Country Club.

Stella Robeson Sleepy Hollow's chef.

Tom MacNulty The country club's bartender.

Luanne Winslow Tom MacNulty's girlfriend.

Billy Birdwell and Tammie Coworkers at the country club.

Cord Stanford Entrepreneur and owner of Stanford Motors.

Jason Bowman An employee of Valley Labs.

Harmon Brinker Owner of The Book Cellar.

Jolee Rodgers Director of Safe Harbor, a home for elderly women.

Rosalie Blumquist Safe Harbor's enigmatic, oldest resident.

CHAPTER ONE

Halloween was once my favorite holiday, but now on the eve of the celebration for departed souls, my own soul, in fact my whole being, was fast filling up with dread. It wasn't that I had anything against ghosts, real or imaginary, or the very-much-alive spirits who bewitch normally intelligent adults into rewarding them with treats in exchange for no trickery. No, the dread came from my realization that October 31 was the projected date for the long-awaited grand reopening of Sleepy Hollow Country Club's main dining room.

"I must have been nuts to take on the project," I said to my audience of two. I really didn't expect Pesty, a five-year-old Keeshond, to express her opinion, but when her yawn matched that of my husband's, Charles William Hastings, it caused me to lose the last of my inherited Irish patience.

"Jesus, Mary, and Joseph," I intoned

grumpily, "nobody in this family feels my pain. Nobody even cares that my reputation as Seville, Indiana's leading interior designer is on the line."

"Oh, come on, Jean. Leading designer?" questioned Charlie, stifling another yawn. "How about Seville's *only* interior designer, unless you want to count the legions of college boys who morph into house painters every summer. And let's not forget old man Wilson. His offer to wall-wash five rooms for fifty bucks still stands, although I hear he's considering expanding his business to include trash removal. Now that's what I call healthy competition — a former janitor and a bunch of frat boys."

Easily extracting himself from the confines of his favorite chair — an ancient, leather recliner — Charlie sat down beside me on the plaid, camelback sofa that dominates our paneled den. The small room is more cozy and inviting than chic.

"Sweetheart, you've got a bad case of opening-night jitters. Trust me, everything is going to be just fine. After tomorrow night, the place will be the talk of the town." Charlie, an opinionated, retired investment counselor expected to be proven right as usual.

Twelve years ago, when I was suffering

12

from empty-nest syndrome, Charlie suggested that I should consider starting a business of my own. It was either that or find a new husband. There is only so much togetherness two people can tolerate, he argued, once the reality of retirement sets in.

Whereas Charlie had both golf and his computer to occupy his time, I'd sought deliverance in the decorating of our home. Once every room had been done and re-done, I began to foist my ideas on friends for free. That people would be willing to pay for my advice and design skills came as a surprise to me, but not to Charlie, and not to our only child and married daughter, Jean junior, better known as JR.

Encouraged by my family, I went back to college and eventually passed the National Council for Interior Design Qualification (NCIDQ) examination. An invitation to join the United Federation of Interior Designers (UFID) followed my graduation. Shortly thereafter, with JR as my helper and junior partner, the firm of Designer Jeans came into being.

Landing the contract with Sleepy Hollow was the high point of what had been a slow spring and an even slower summer. Now on the eve of the reopening I, Jean Hastings, a woman who had gone through the ordeal of

13

giving birth, earning a college degree post menopause, and surviving my husband's early retirement was on the verge of a full-blown panic attack. If I had overstated my position in the community, as Charlie insinuated, then so be it. I had finally gotten his undivided attention.

"Dear," said Charlie in a most condescending tone, "do you remember what Theodore Roosevelt said when he led his men up San Juan Hill?"

Curious to hear my husband's latest take on historical trivia I shrugged, feigning ignorance.

"According to Teddy, the only thing you have to fear is fear itself," Charlie informed me, immensely pleased with himself.

"You don't say. Then maybe it was Mrs. Roosevelt who yelled Charge! Do you suppose she was shopping in Havana at the time?" I'd replaced self-pity with sarcasm.

Charlie raised his hands in a gesture of mock surrender. "Okay, I give up. Maybe I don't know much about history, but I do know how hard you and JR worked on the project. And I also know you got the job in the first place because you're a talented designer. Just look at Valhalla." This was Charlie's special name for Vernon and Vanessa Higgins's palatial home. "People rave about the place, thanks to you."

Helping me up from the sofa, Charlie suggested we check out our own Valhalla. "It's pretty late and I've got an early morning tee time. Maybe what you really should be worried about is how you're going to convince me to wear a costume to the shindig tomorrow night."

"Oh jeez," I moaned, rolling my eyes as we made our way up the staircase to the master bedroom. With all the fretting about the project, I'd forgotten that the club's board had voted on a costume dinner dance for the reopening. Since the date coincided with Halloween, going in costume made sense. At least, it had at the time. Later, probably because of a myriad of unexpected scheduling and budget problems, the costume bit had completely slipped my mind.

Catching a glimpse of myself in the hall mirror, I facetiously remarked that perhaps I should go to the affair as a bag lady. Since he's a smart husband, Charlie wisely said nothing.

Donning an oversized official Indianapolis Colts tee shirt, I slid comfortably into the brass four-poster bed and collided lightly with my husband. Safe and snug in the arms of my high school sweetheart, all thoughts

15

of costumes and country clubs had vanished.

"Oh boy," said Charlie, "wait 'til the guys find out that I had great sex with a bag lady."

Deliberately pressing my cold feet against his bare legs, I warned him not to discuss the subject with his golf cronies. "You say one word, and I'll tell Vanessa Higgins that you want the first dance with her."

Knowing how much he disliked both dancing and Vanessa, I had my husband just where I wanted him. It made for a nice night.

By seven o'clock the next morning, I was on the phone with JR. I figured that with a set of eight-year-old twins, a cop husband, and a menagerie of animals, my thirtysomething daughter would be up and ready for the day.

"Mother," she answered in a voice with a familiar edge (a holdover from her teenaged years), "what in God's name is so damn important that you felt compelled to call me at this ungodly hour?"

Trying to make my own voice sound authoritative and motherly, I replied, "I need your help."

"Help? What kind of help? I thought we were all done at the club. All that's left to do is to show up for the damn dinner dance.

16

Oh no, you didn't book us for another job today, did you?"

Before I had a chance to answer, JR rushed on. "You know Matt's not crazy about my working so many hours as it is, plus I've got to be at school for a parent-teacher conference at three o'clock today. I'm fresh out of cereal and dog food, and Kerry's stitches are supposed to be taken out at four, and I haven't seen our cat since the twins tried to give it a bath last night. And if all that isn't enough, I promised to take the kids trick-or-treating before the sitter gets here tonight. So what's your problem?"

"Hey JR, don't bite my head off. Can I help it if the Seville Police Department doesn't pay its best cop more money, and Chief Stevens refuses to retire thus keeping Matt from officially taking over?" Even though everything I said was the truth, I had only brought up Matt Cusak's (my son-in-law of twelve years), employment woes in an effort to put an end to JR's tirade. Usually, she is more than willing to discuss the subject, but not this time.

"Mother," JR yelled into the phone, "Chief Stevens is not going to be responsible for Kelly and Kerry being late for school today, but their goofy grandmother is. If you're

17

worried about my picking up the three tarps, paint brushes, and roller pan, I promise I'll get them out of the club's storeroom before the grand reopening."

"That's fine," I said, aware that I had about ten seconds or less to explain myself. "What I need are some costume ideas for your father. I've just about given up on him. As for me, I might go as a bag lady. What do you think?"

"I think you've finally lost it. Pops warned me yesterday not to get involved. With your talent for design, I'm sure you'll come up with something special for him. And since you asked, forget the bag lady thing. It hits too close to home. Have you given any thought to a complete makeover? Some lip gloss, mascara, henna rinse, and a push-up bra can do wonders, even for a woman your age."

I had only myself to blame for my daughter's innate sense of humor.

"Gotta go, Mom. Love ya. See you tonight. Good luck with Pops and the costumes." JR rang off, leaving me with a cold telephone and an even colder cup of coffee.

"Well Pesty, old gal, I guess it's just you and me against the Charlie Hastings of the world. You got any good ideas? Food for thought?"

The word *food* brought the lounging Kees to her feet. With her ears up and tongue out, Pesty stared at the pantry cabinet, silently commanding the door to open.

CHAPTER TWO

"Sweetie," Vanessa Higgins had said in her syrupy voice, "Ah just know y'all and lil' what's-her-name can handle the teensy job of redoin' our club's main dinin' room. Why, y'all did a right smashin' job on VanVern Manor. Even after all these years, the place still looks mighty fine."

Instead of concentrating on finding a solution for the costume problem, I'd turned to woolgathering, recalling Vanessa's unexpected visit to Kettle Cottage three months ago. Despite the passage of time, her positive remarks regarding Designer Jeans were still fresh in my memory.

It was hard to believe that five years had passed since JR and I had taken on the project of redecorating VanVern Manor, aka the old Higgins place. The Italianate-style house with a wraparound porch, arched windows, and square tower was built in the 1870s by Garrison Seville, Civil War hero and founder of our town. Garrison and his wife, Betsy, wanted a place grand enough to impress visitors and roomy enough to accommodate their five children. Sadly, only one, a boy named Tad, survived the diphtheria that took the lives of his siblings.

As a young man, Tad rebelled against his pampered, sheltered childhood. After joining a secondrate, traveling vaudeville show, he married the headstrong Fern Wilde (a preacher's daughter), in a shotgun ceremony. The marriage was an open one with the participants each going their own way.

The couple's only child, Verna, was born seven months after the wedding. Because of her parents' rather Bohemian lifestyle, the girl was raised primarily by her grandparents, Garrison and Betsy. Alcoholism eventually took the lives of both of her parents, making the orphaned Verna the sole heir to the fortune Garrison had made in a series of extremely profitable land deals.

When the beautiful girl reached adulthood, the entire town held its collective breath, waiting to see if Verna was going to emulate the unorthodox behavior of her parents and thumb her nose at conventional morals. If that's what they expected, then the prim and proper Verna disappointed them. The young woman married Grant

Higgins, the owner of a growing chain of drugstores. The ceremony was private and attended by close family and friends, most of whom were out-of-towners.

It was rumored that perhaps the young heiress had married down. This proved to be untrue. Grant came from one of Boston's richest, oldest, and most respected families. By the time their son, Vernon, was born in the spring of 1930, Grant had parlayed his holdings into Valley Labs, a giant in the pharmaceuticals industry. The privately owned conglomerate became (and still is), Seville's largest employer. Most of Valley's workers are lifetime employees and lifetime residents of Seville.

Less than a hundred miles from Indianapolis, Seville offers a pace akin to that of the rural South. It is unlike the state capital, which reflects the urban hustle and bustle most often associated with the thriving industrial cities of the North. That's not to say our town is slow or backward, because it isn't. Despite its small size (the population is slightly over twenty thousand), Seville has some of the finest schools in the state of Indiana. An award-winning journalist, a United State Supreme Court Justice, and a popular screen idol all claimed Seville as their hometown. This comes as a surprise only to those who have never spent time in our little metropolis.

Not that everyone from Seville whose name ends up in the history books, or on the front page of the newspaper, is of sterling character. We've had our share of the infamous as well as the famous.

In 1913, Hetty Fox hacked her lover to death and fed his remains to the pigs. The whole sordid story made its way up to Chicago and beyond. For awhile, it looked like it was going to be turned into a movie, but the man in charge decided to film a more encompassing tale, and Hetty's story was scrapped. When Griffith's *The Birth of a Nation* was released in 1915, everyone in Seville agreed that D. W. had made the right decision.

In the late 1920s, Finky Dee, a former Chicago mobster-turned-Indiana casino owner, was bumped off in his office and his killer was never caught.

During War II, G-men raided an old abandoned flour mill not five miles out of town and broke up a black-market operation dealing in counterfeit ration coupons. Everyone was shocked when the gang's leader turned out to be the head of Seville's town council. His portrait was promptly removed from all public buildings, including the police station. He ended up serving more time in prison than he'd served on the council.

Occasionally we lose some of our young people to big cities such as Indianapolis, Chicago, St. Louis, and Cincinnati, yet most of these adventurous souls eventually return to Seville, where family ties are as solid as the winter ice on Fox's Pond and as strong as the summer sun that bakes the open farmland. With the latest technological advancements available to the entire community, Seville, Indiana, is about as modern a place to live as Kansas City where, according to a certain Broadway show tune, everything is up to date.

Seville takes pride in its past, which includes great examples of mid- and late-nineteenth-century architecture. Many of the houses and commercial buildings from the period have been modernized and converted into apartments, shops, or office complexes. Others, such as VanVern Manor, have managed to retain much of their original splendor and charm. When the widowed Verna passed away, Vernon inherited everything, including the old mansion.

Five years ago, after a whirlwind courtship conducted mostly in Indianapolis where Vanessa was based as a flight attendant for Southern Cross Airlines, the May/December couple tied the knot. As a wedding present for his young bride, Vernon hired Designer Jeans to redecorate the mansion's formal parlor. Since Vanessa saw herself as the hostess with the mostest, it was imperative that the parlor be a suitable one in which to entertain important guests. After settling on a design plan that virtually gave Designer Jeans a free hand, the project was under way.

To be honest, I have to admit the VanVern project was as great a financial success as it was a professional one for Designer Jeans. With JR's help and Vernon's money, it wasn't too hard to transform the cold, uninviting formal parlor into a warm and welcoming room.

We began by removing everything, including a gigantic screen, console TV that had usurped the fireplace as the main focal point, out of the room. Then, we painted the walls and ceiling in a pale shade of terra cotta with an eggshell finish. The warm, soft color called attention to the golden oak crown molding and baseboard trim. Next, the honey-colored hardwood floor was revived with a plethora of wax and elbow grease.

When most of what JR refers to as grunt

work was out of the way, I had a licensed electrician install a trio of downlights above the massive fireplace. The recessed lighting, a pair of opalescent table lamps, and a well-placed floor lamp would bathe the room in an ambient glow.

With natural light at a premium, we decided to dress the parlor's single window (a tall, narrow, arched opening), from ceiling to floor in a billowy, white lace curtain with generous side panels of buttery, yellow taffeta. It was an easy solution to a problematic architectural element.

A cozy conversation area was created using a contemporary-style celery green, damask-covered sofa; a pair of club chairs done in a striped chenille of soft orange, yellow, and beige; and an oversized, caramel-colored leather ottoman-cum-coffee table. The new furniture, along with Garrison Seville's writing table and Betsy Seville's sewing stand (original parlor pieces), was arranged asymmetrically atop a newly purchased oriental rug. The rug's dominant colors of persimmon, deep gold, and chocolate brown complemented the warm, analogous color scheme called for in the agreed-upon design plan.

Just off to the side of the conversation area, we grouped a green leather Stickley chair; a small tea table; and a modestly proportioned armoire in an intimate semi-circle. The cabinet housed a new plasma high-definition TV set.

A sleek, mahogany sideboard with mirror (circa 1918), was rescued from the mansion's attic. Positioned against the wall opposite the fireplace, the sideboard balanced the room. It also provided a convenient staging area for drinks and snacks.

Some vanilla satin pillows here, a fresh floral arrangement there, and the project was finished on time and only slightly over budget.

Standing in front of the fireplace, JR and I accepted Vernon's check and kudos for a job well done. Even the bride, whose sophomoric taste in home decor had threatened to derail the project on more than one occasion, was pleased. And pleasing the self-absorbed woman was not an easy matter.

From the day she arrived in Seville, Vanessa Higgins had managed to alienate almost everyone in town with the exception of her husband and the blockheads who elected her president of Sleepy Hollow's board of directors.

Before long, Vanessa was running roughshod over her fellow board members: Harmon Brinker, owner of a bookstore; Jason

Bowman, a Valley Lab chemist; and Cord Stanford, an enterprising car dealer.

When Vanessa wanted something, she knew how to get it. Using a combination of femininity, clout, and Southern charm seldom found this side of the Mason-Dixon Line, she saw to it that the redecorating of the country club's main dining room topped the board's priority list, much to the dismay of Harrison Fowler, Sleepy Hollow's new manager.

None of this was known to me at the time of Vanessa's unexpected visit. Like a cluster of falling leaves, she swirled into my kitchen office with an offer no struggling interior designer could refuse: the chance to turn a tidy profit along with the opportunity for some always-welcome positive PR.

"Now sweetie," said Vanessa, "it's all settled then. Ah'd surely appreciate it if y'all and lil' what's-her-name would begin immediately."

Screwing her meticulously painted mouth into an attractive pout, Vanessa frowned prettily. "It's very importin' that those of us used to better not be inconvenienced any longer than absolutely necessary."

Since my mouth was already open, I figured I might as well try to get in some sort of reply. "I thought you said Harrison was going to extend the club's bar and grill hours during the time when the dining room will be closed down."

"Oh, he will darlin' but the bar and grill is so, so . . . oh, what's that word Ah need? Common. Y'all know what Ah'm sayin'?" drawled the former flight attendant. "It's definitely not first class. The place is usually just crawlin' with those golfers and the like." She made it sound as though golfers were the scourge rather than the backbone of the country club.

With her mission accomplished, Vanessa took her leave, pausing only long enough to give Pesty an obligatory pat on the head.

Feeling like the old, faithful servant witnessing the departure of her mistress, I latched the bottom half of the Dutch door with one hand and waved a hearty goodbye with the other. From over my shoulder a masculine voice called out to the fast-retreating figure, "Hey, and a big thank y'all for visitin' with us common folk. It's been a real hoot, y'all know what Ah'm sayin'?"

"Shame on you Charlie for eavesdropping," I scolded. "And get that silly grin off your face. She might have heard you." But honestly, I really wasn't upset or surprised by his reaction to Vanessa's remarks.

"I doubt if she did. Her Highness was too

busy brushing doggy hair off her derriere to notice anything or anybody. Lordy, how ever will she survive the terrible ordeal of eating with the hoi polloi? Maybe Fowler could add little packages of peanuts to the menu. Or hand out sack lunches. Anything to make our Vanessa comfy."

I could tell that Charlie was warming to the subject. Next, he'd be making smart remarks about burp bags, call buttons, and miniscule meals served on plastic trays.

"Charlie, go catch up on your e-mail or something. I've got an awful lot to do in a very short time. Nine weeks may seem like an eternity to some people, but to those of us who paint and patch for a living, the time will just fly by. No pun intended," I added quickly in an effort to stave off any further comments related to the former occupation of the current Mrs. Vernon Higgins.

Confusing the word *pun* with the word *bun,* Pesty looked around the kitchen for some sign of a pastry treat. When nothing in the way of food materialized, she whined in protest.

Ignoring both the dog and her master, I cleared the kitchen table, pulled out my workbooks, and began the important task of assembling the schedule and scheme needed for Designer Jeans's newest project.

CHAPTER THREE

Built in the late 1920s by Francis Dertz, a.k.a. Finky Dee, the Sleepy Hollow clubhouse was originally designed as a posh gambling casino. Architecturally, it was pure early-twentieth-century California kitsch, complete with a white stucco exterior, arched porticos, and an orange-colored tile roof. Critics (and there were more than a few) sniffed that the place looked like two giant steamer trunks joined in the middle by a hat box. Maybe so, but it didn't seem to bother Finky or his customers, many of whom drove all the way from Chicago to see, and be seen in, what had quickly become the Hoosier State's hottest night spot.

Finky was basically an okay guy who fell in with the wrong crowd in Chicago. When his bullet-riddled body was discovered in his Sleepy Hollow office on October 24, 1929, Finky's demise was overshadowed by the death of America's economy. The fact that Roxy Bloom, Finky's part-time hostess and sometime mistress, was missing along with the murder weapon led the local gendarme to conclude that Roxy was the perpetrator of the crime.

As the entire country became enveloped in the era known as the Great Depression, Finky's murder and Roxy's subsequent disappearance gradually faded into welcomed oblivion. Seville's residents were more concerned with unemployment, bankruptcies, evictions, and foreclosures than what had become of Finky's killer. Besides, the general consensus was that the unsavory casino owner had probably done the missing Roxy wrong and he simply got what he deserved.

Throughout the 1930s the casino stood empty and unsold despite its low price, but the entry of the United States into World War II in 1941 brought renewed interest in the property. After a stint as Seville's Servicemen's Canteen, the old place, along with its surrounding acreage, was purchased by a cartel of local businessmen.

What followed was the transformation of corn fields into a private eighteen-hole golf course. The former casino became a clubhouse complete with a formal dining room, bar and grill, full kitchen, storage room, locker facilities, and manager's office. Despite a rather hefty fee charged for the privilege of joining, the monthly dues, green fees, food and drink, and the occasional assessment have remained relatively low.

The west wing's bar and grill had to be completely redone a few years ago due to damaged caused by a suspicious fire. Since the east wing and the rotunda hadn't suffered any damage, the rooms in that wing, along with the rotunda's dining room, were not rebuilt, remodeled, or updated.

The disparities between the old and new sections of the clubhouse were hard to ignore. This was especially true of the bar and grill and the main dining room. While the former had been splendidly modernized and decorated, the latter had received only the proverbial lick and a promise.

That the once-grand old room needed much more became obvious in the cold light of day when, with one strong tug on a frayed drapery cord, the entire window treatment came crashing down on JR's head, pushing her to the floor.

"Jeez, what happened JR? Good lord girl, answer me." Panicking, I inadvertently knocked over the stack of metal folding chairs that had been resting against the wall.

The sound of metal crashing against metal made a horrendous din as the chairs, like the walls of Jericho, came tumbling down. I ignored the noise and continued to race across the room before snagging the heel of my shoe on the matted shag carpeting. Thrown off balance, I reached out for the nearest object, which was a large, dried-out potted palm. With plant in tow, I crash-landed on the mound of drapery, which had imprisoned JR. My rescue attempt, needless to say, was a fiasco.

"Mother, get off," came the muffled voice. "I can't breathe. You're squishing me."

I rolled to the side, a move that gave JR enough room to crawl out from under the odious stained and sun-rotted fabric. Once we'd untangled ourselves from the debris and were back on our feet, I instructed JR to take it easy while I cleaned up the mess, but she assured me that, other than a temporary loss of breath and a slight bump on her head, she was fine.

"You took quite a spill yourself, Mom. I didn't see it, but I sure felt it. You didn't hurt anything, did you?"

"Only my dignity. Although I survived, I don't think the same can be said for the drapes or the potted palm," I said, removing bits of both from my face and mouth.

"It's a good thing I wasn't planning on using them in the makeover."

What happened next was neither planned, nor a good thing; at that moment the club manager, Harrison Fowler, decided to make an appearance.

"What in hell is going on in here? Who are you people?" demanded Harrison as he entered the room. His face was red with anger. "Just look at this mess! Why, you've practically ruined the place."

Obviously, the first meeting between Designer Jeans and Sleepy Hollow's new manager was off to a bad start. Clad as we were in painter caps and coveralls, Harrison Fowler hadn't recognized us as the interior designers. After a brief reintroduction, followed by an even briefer explanation, we found ourselves accompanying the man to his east wing office.

Stepping inside the room was like stepping back in time. As a first-time visitor to what had been Finky Dee's private lair, I was struck by its opulence. All the innovated design elements associated with the Art Deco era remained virtually untouched and intact.

We were directed to a pair of accent chairs covered in black leather and gleaming chrome trim. The low-slung chairs were positioned in front of an elevated ebony desk. Like everything else in the room, the business area had been beautifully designed and executed, right down to black-and-gold-embossed leather desk accessories and a banker's lamp of brass and green glass.

Before taking his place, Harrison removed a heavily perfumed letter, a vinyl packet, and a dog-eared passbook from the inside pocket of his sport coat. He carefully placed the items in the middle drawer of the massive desk. While he was getting settled in, I was busy soaking up the room's decor.

Despite the early hour, sconces with delicate fan-shaped alabaster shades had been turned on and were throwing waves of artificial light across oak-paneled walls. Windows of wavy glass blocks served their original purpose of providing both natural light and privacy. The richly veined black marble floor was complemented by two well-placed Persian rugs. The curved ceiling's mural had darkened with time, yet the Manhattan skyline it depicted was still visible, illuminated by a large circular crystal-beaded chandelier. At the far end of the room, a heavily fringed, iridescent silk-covered chaise lounge could be seen just beyond the partially opened Oriental screen. A stark-white baby grand piano, and a mirrored, U-shaped cocktail bar completed the stunning decor.

Thoroughly entranced, I'd failed to pay attention to matters at hand until I became aware of the manager's penetrating stare as he repeated his question.

"Mrs. Hastings, do you understand the point I've been trying to make?" The tone of his voice indicated a growing impatience. "Sleepy Hollow Country Club, regardless of what Vanessa, er, Mrs. Higgins, might have led you to believe, does not have an unlimited budget to work with on this project. Personally, I'm of the opinion that the funds set aside for it would be better spent on repaving the parking lot. Judging from my records, in spite of the numerous changes that I've made in both the food and the hours, the formal dining room generates very little business."

"Perhaps that's because it also generates very little ambiance," JR shot back a tad too sharply. "Half the swag lamps don't work, the window coverings are a disgrace, the flocked wallpaper is starting to peel, and the shag carpeting is atrocious. Face it, Mr. Fowler, the room doesn't attract diners, it repels them."

JR's assessment was spontaneous, honest, and right on target. Harrison Fowler was not about to agree, but he had enough savvy to try a different approach.

"Oh, don't get me wrong, ladies. I happen to agree with Van, er, Mrs. Higgins." Harrison shifted in his chair, taking care not to wrinkle his cashmere sport coat. "The dining room could do with a bit of sprucing up. But come on, how much can a couple gallons of paint cost? Hell, you can rent one of those rug cleaning machines for a few bucks. As for the drapes, they probably can be repaired. Same goes for the lights. Let's face it, the whole job could be done over a weekend, maybe two, and for considerably less money."

When I politely disagreed and suggested that perhaps he didn't comprehend the magnitude of the dining room's problems, the man's demeanor changed completely. No longer smiling, Harrison Fowler leaned forward and shook his fist, first at JR and then at me.

"Listen to me and listen good. I don't know exactly what you two broads have in mind, but remember this — I'll be right here making damn sure you don't go one day over schedule, or one dollar over budget. Is that clear?"

"Perfectly clear, Mr. Fowler," I said, resisting the urge to reach across the desk and deliver a well-deserved slap to his face. "Now it's your turn to listen. As members of this club, we don't work for you, you work for us. Designer Jeans was hired by the club's board to redecorate the dining room, which, in effect, means we are working for ourselves. Designer Jeans is a reputable firm with an impeccable reputation. We have never cheated a customer on time, labor, or materials. I suggest you back off, chum, before Designer Jeans decides to sue you for slander and the board for breach of contract. How's that for being clear?"

I signaled to JR that we were leaving. Harrison Fowler's mouth hung open. If he had a reply, it'd gotten lost somewhere between his brain and tongue. At times, the fifty-something bachelor bore a resemblance to the late actor Zachary Scott. This was not one of those times. "Close your mouth, Harrison, you look foolish. Come on JR, I'll buy you a cup of coffee in the bar and grill, where the air is fresher and the staff is friendlier." My sometimes-arthritic knee cooperated, allowing me to make a swift exit.

Pausing in the doorway of the office, JR grabbed hold of my arm, causing me to stop abruptly. "Mother, do you realize what you just said?" she scolded, her lovely face only inches from my own. "You know I don't drink coffee."

CHAPTER FOUR

After seeing the manager's office, JR agreed with me. The inspiration for the project would be the club's original Art Deco decor. Using some modern techniques and good planning, I felt we could reintroduce the style and feel of the era in the dining room's makeover. The trick would be to do so without blowing the budget or schedule. Time, more than money, would prove to be our biggest stumbling block.

As the days grew shorter, the hours spent removing layer upon layer of old paint and wallpaper grew longer. Occasionally, our work was interrupted by visits from various board members. Like her father, JR does not suffer fools gladly or quietly. Overtired one day, she was voicing her frustration as she struggled with a particularly hard-to-remove section of paper.

"If one more of those yahoos stops by just to tell me that I missed a spot, I swear somebody's going to wind up dead."

Before I had a chance to offer JR some much-needed sympathy along with some well-deserved praise for the terrific job she was doing, Harmon Brinker toddled into the dining room, ducking easily beneath the latticework of scaffolding.

"Dead you say. Oh my, my, my." The corpulent bachelor's eyelids fluttered as he spoke. "It mustn't happen here in the club. Or to someone we know. Given the choice, I'd rather it be a stranger; otherwise, I'll have to close the shop for the funeral. The timing would be awful. Business is already slow, what with this dreadful Indian summer and all."

Harmon paused to mop his round face with a monogrammed sweat-soaked, linen handkerchief. "Since death is inevitable, doesn't that make every death, regardless of the circumstances, a natural occurrence? And the only sorrow therefore, would be that it happened sooner rather than later. I myself prefer brevity over the long goodbye, which, for reasons most peculiar, is favored by some. Often they are the very same people who, when death finally does come, are not willing to accept it for what it is: the cessation of existence. It is that and nothing more than that. Wouldn't you agree? Or am

I wrong?"

Harmon carefully folded the damp square of cloth before making a second pass over his face. "One can't help but admire Oscar Wilde's approach to death. As an interior designer, you probably appreciate his dying words better than most. But that's neither here nor there. Isn't it high time we allowed the old dog to rest in peace? What's past is past, and what's dead is gone. We sometimes must accept the unacceptable, even when we find it to be offensive. Isn't that so, Mrs. Hastings?"

What one thing had to do with the other had me confused, yet mixing up phrases, people, and events seemed to make perfect sense to the rotund, elfinlike bookseller. The conversation was classic Harmon.

Harmon Brinker's family fled the Netherlands one step ahead of the 1940 Nazi invasion of the Low Countries. After a short stay in England, Harmon's parents and their teenaged daughter made the long trek to the United States via Canada. The family eventually settled in Seville, where Harmon was born.

The Brinkers managed a successful bulb farm, and in their spare time, doted on their son. The daughter left home shortly before the end of World War II. Supposedly she returned to Amsterdam, where she married a Nazi sympathizer. This was something that wasn't verified, or denied, by the Brinkers, who never spoke of their daughter's departure and treated Harmon as if he were their only child.

Harmon's formative years were marred by a barrage of hurtful teasing directed at him by town bullies. Because of his small stature and Dutch heritage, young Harmon had to endure nicknames such as "Pansy," "Wooden Shoes," and "Herman the German." The last one (and according to Harmon, the most hurtful), was inspired by his sister's absence.

It is said that time heals all wounds. With the passage of time, a seemingly healed Harmon Brinker accepted the people of Seville, and they in turn accepted the fussy, permanently befuddled, decidedly feminine, little man.

"Harmon, come sit down before you pass out. JR will get you a cold can of soda. You can relax. Nobody's dead or going to die soon, at least not while the two Jeans are on the job." Taking the can of soda that JR had retrieved from the nearby portable ice chest, I popped the tab and passed the open can to our perturbed visitor.

He thanked me for the soda and the chair.

"Oh my, my," he said to JR as she plopped down on the floor beside him, "you're looking more like your daddy everyday, but I'll bet you're smart like your mama, even though she has a tendency to involve herself in difficult situations. Isn't that always the case when one is a problem solver and truth seeker?"

With a blink of his long eyelashes and a flash of a smile, Harmon wiggled around in an effort to find a comfortable position, something virtually impossible to do when seated on a bent, metal folding chair.

"Oh dear me, I don't suppose you ladies have any straws. No problem though, this will do fine. Yes, fine. We all must get used to things not being the way we would like them to be. As others must do, so shall I." Then, as if to prove his point, Harmon winked and took a dainty sip from the soda can.

Because of the convoluted nature of Harmon's style of conversation, I made no attempt to answer any of the little man's questions. Neither did JR.

While I continued to silently sort through the maze of Harmon's words, JR's infectious giggle filled the room. Setting her painter's cap at a jaunty angle, she inched closer to the clearly uncomfortable Harmon

Brinker.

"Why Mr. Brinker, are you flirting with me or is it really my mother you're after? Come on, tell me the truth. However, as the wife of a cop, I must remind you that anything you say in your defense can be used against you in the court of public opinion."

For a fraction of a second, I thought I saw a hint of anger in the little man's watery blue eyes. Or was it fear? I couldn't be sure. "Okay JR, I think Mr. Brinker has had enough of Designer Jeans for one day. We mustn't keep him from whatever it is that brings him to the club on such a warm October afternoon."

I must confess that I was curious as to the purpose of his visit since according to *Hollow Greetings,* the club's monthly newsletter, the board wasn't scheduled to meet until the first of November, which was still some weeks away.

For the moment, Harmon seemed at a loss for words. "Oh silly me," he finally stammered, "I came for one of the new cook's fantastic Cobb salads. You can imagine my embarrassment when I realized today is Monday. Why, everyone in town knows the club is always closed on Mondays. Aren't I the silly one?"

The foppish Harmon, like the white rabbit from Carroll's *Alice in Wonderland,* checked his watch and scurried from the room, mumbling something about being too late. He never even said goodbye. Somewhere down the east corridor, the sound of footsteps could be heard, followed by the noise of a door slamming.

"Curiousor and curiousor," I remarked more to myself than to JR whose enthusiasm for the renovation project at hand had dropped to a new low and was about to drop even lower.

"What? His visit? Or the man himself?" JR said, shooing away a pesky ladybug that had worked its way into the folds of her coveralls.

"Both," I conceded. What was really curious was Harmon's explanation regarding the purpose of his visit to the club. He wasn't the type to close up shop in the middle of the day, and certainly not for a Cobb salad.

"Don't hurt the ladybug, JR. I hear they bring good luck, and I have a feeling that before we're finished with this room we're going to need it."

"Well then," JR announced grimly, inspecting the mountain of supplies we had accumulated in order to transform the room from bland to grand, "you'll be happy to know she's not alone. She's got a whole colony of friends. Yeech!"

With scraper in hand, JR reluctantly returned to the chore, which Harmon's visit had interrupted. "By the way, what did Oscar Wilde have to say about dying or death? I hope it's easier to understand than what Mr. Brinker had to say on the subject."

"It is. Unlike Harmon, Oscar Wilde didn't waste words," I said, closing the windows in a futile attempt to stem the insect invasion. "The great writer and wit was about to breathe his last when he supposedly made the remark that either the wallpaper had to go, or he would. And he did."

CHAPTER FIVE

The following day, I learned of Harmon Brinker's death. According to the local radio report, Harmon's body was discovered on the floor of The Book Cellar earlier that morning by a premed student who, by all accounts, had almost died himself from the shock of the reality of death. Upon hearing the news, I phoned Matt down at police headquarters in hopes of getting a more detailed report. After listening to the usual lecture about minding my own business, my son-in-law threw a few crumbs my way, including the fact that Patti Crump, the first police officer on the scene, took one look at the gory mess and promptly passed out cold.

While alone in his store, sometime between eight and nine o'clock in the morning, Harmon had climbed up the tall library ladder. Apparently he'd been reaching for one of the leather-bound books on the top shelf and lost his balance. His fall was broken by a three-foot-high bronze statue of Lady Macbeth, a recent acquisition from an online auction. As with her other victims, the lady showed Harmon no mercy. Her outstretched hands were covered with his blood, and what remained of the booksell-er's brains lay splattered at her feet. Matt was insistent that the death was an accident — perhaps a bit too insistent. That, coupled with his flat delivery of the facts, added to my own suspicion that Lady Macbeth wasn't the only one with bloody hands.

WNEW, an Indianapolis television station, covered the death on the nightly news, call-ing it a freak accident. The camera panned the large crowd that had gathered on the sidewalk in front of the bookstore. Gasps could be heard when the gurney with the body was loaded into the back of the ambu-lance for the short ride to Garrison General where Harmon was pronounced dead on arrival. The coverage ended with the re-porter cheerily advising everyone to stay tuned for the latest in sports and weather.

The general public, and the authorities, accepted the who, what, and where of Har-mon's death. What bothered me was the how and why. In spite of what he'd said about briefness, I didn't believe that Harmon would have preferred such a sudden, violent end over a slow, natural death. But what I did believe was that someone made the decision for him.

I attended the simple graveside service, as did Harmon's fellow board members: Vanessa Higgins, Jason Bowman, and Cord Stanford. Harrison Fowler, Chief Stevens, and Hilly Murrow (the reporter for our local newspaper) showed up as well. While there was a scarcity of mourners, there was an abundance of flowers. Hilly was quick to inform me that the expensive floral arrangements were sent by the pot-smoking college boys who used The Book Cellar as a free coffeehouse.

Without any family or clergy present (Harmon was an agnostic), it fell to the senior Mr. Twall of Twall and Sons Mortuary to deliver the eulogy. The elderly funeral director checked over his notes before giving a nearly flawless reading of Robert Frost's "Bereft." Harmon had left instructions with his lawyer that Ezra Pound's "Cantos" be read, but supposedly no copy of the lengthy, controversial work could be located. (I guess it didn't occur to the lawyer, or the Twalls, to check The Book Cellar.) All and all, I thought things went about as well as could be expected under the circumstances, and Harmon would have been satisfied.

Once the service was over, Jason Bowman appeared at my side and began a monologue about life's trials and tribulations. I was anxious to get in my van and out of the thigh-high nylon hosiery I'd worn. Like the rest of my outfit, the stockings were better suited for a walk on a cold winter's night than a trek through a cemetery on a warm, Indian summer's day. I listened politely to Jason's prattle before handing him off to Vanessa and slipping away. I caught up with Rollie Stevens in time to hear him give a rather Shakespearean statement to the press.

When asked by the aggressive Hilly about Harmon's sudden demise, the police chief replied, "Although the manner of death contained both sound and fury, Mr. Brinker's death was one of those unfortunate accidents. As such, there's nothing that can or will be done. Officially, the case is over. Harmon Brinker's death, like his life, is kaput."

Rollie Stevens was being his usual maddening self. He turned to me, rolled his eyes, and smiled. A sudden gust of wind sent a cold chill down my spine. Had she been there, my mother would've said it was a sign that someone was walking on my grave.

In my haste to get away, I unintentionally trampled over the final resting place of a number of the dearly departed. As I tripped over yet another stone marker, I came to the conclusion that whoever came up with the idea of ground-level monuments deserved to be buried alive under a mound of fallen leaves, grass clippings, and broken shoe heels.

When I reached the van, I climbed inside, started the motor, and switched on the air conditioner. Pleased to find that the thigh high nylons hadn't completed bonded to my skin, I discreetly raised my skirt, pulled off the stockings, and bathed my legs in the cool air. Enjoying the moment, my thoughts turned to Harmon. Perhaps he had something to do with the continuation of the hot, humid weather. Maybe it was his way of paying society back for, as the chief put it, "an unfortunate accident." I hadn't a clue as to what really happened on that fateful morning in The Book Cellar, but whatever it was that Rollie Stevens was selling, I wasn't buying it.

CHAPTER SIX

By now, I'd gathered enough wool to clothe the naked of the earth and then some. While the memories of the Van Vern project, Vanessa's unexpected visit, the redo of the club's dining room, and Harmon's death were interesting, they did nothing to solve my costume dilemma.

Returning the cordless telephone to its base on the shiny black granite countertop, and my mind to the present, I ignored Pesty's pleas for a jelly doughnut.

"You ought to be glad you don't live at JR's. She doesn't feed her pets; she just loses them."

My daughter was too harried to be bothered, and my husband was totally uncooperative, so I passed the role of adviser to Pesty. In spite of giving me her full attention, the Kees had nothing to say. I might as well have been talking to myself, which I was doing when Charlie sauntered into the kitchen.

"Good morning, sweetheart. Don't let me interrupt your conversation. By the way, do you know that talking to one's self, like smoking, is not the healthiest of habits? If you don't believe me, ask Pesty."

Dressed for a day on the links, Charlie helped himself to a cup of coffee and a nut-encrusted pastry before sitting down to await the arrival of his brother-in-law and golf partner, Denny England.

"Better yet, ask Doc Parker. You might also ask him about the patch. It worked for me. Haven't had a smoke in over a year," he bragged. Breaking off a small piece of the sweet roll, Charlie tossed the morsel to Pesty, who devoured it in less than a New York minute.

Frustration over my family's lack of concern regarding my costume dilemma had been percolating inside of me. Heated by JR's flippancy, and stirred by my husband's attempt to put me on the defensive, it came to a boil when Charlie shared his breakfast with the dog.

"Charlie Hastings, what do you think you're doing? The doctors at the animal clinic told you that Pesty has to lose some weight or she's going to end up being wider than she is tall. Remember? No more people food. Besides, the nuts are bad for her digestion. They give her gas."

Aware that she was in the eye of a potential marital storm, Pesty hunkered down under the round oak table.

"Don't change the subject," said Charlie, licking a smidgen of frosting from his thumb. "We were discussing your problem, not the dog's. Are you worried about gaining weight if you stop smoking? Well, don't. On you, it would look good."

"Hey, Charlie," Denny England called out, leaning through the open top half of the kitchen's Dutch door, "you better watch what you say. The last time I kidded your sister about her weight, she served nothing but rice cakes and salad for a month. Now everything in our house is fat-free 'cept Mary."

Actually, neither Denny's nor Mary's weight has changed much since the day this Jack Spratt couple married thirty-five years ago. Laughing at his own joke, the lanky Denny unlatched the lower portion of the door and ushered himself into the room.

With his ruddy complexion, a fringe of steely gray hair, and crinkly blue eyes, Denny looks as though he should be behind the wheel of a ship rather than selling furniture in landlocked Seville, Indiana. As a young man, he served four years in the navy and claims that he was seasick for the entire 1,461 days. Should some doubting Thomas challenge his claim, Denny has a ready answer: He enlisted on the twenty-ninth of February. About the only thing Denny takes seriously is golf. In spite of giving Charlie a stroke-per-hole advantage, the jovial merchant of fine furniture almost always wins the match. This is something that drives my less-than-jovial, competitive husband a wee bit nuts.

Taking the last of the pastries from the plate on the counter, Denny broke the gooey bun into two pieces, offering the largest portion to the waiting Pesty.

"Hold it right there, chum. Don't you dare give that dog any food." Almost before I had the words out of my mouth, the Kees had half a jelly doughnut in hers. Using her tongue, she delicately retrieved a dollop of the sweet, red filling from the tip of her nose.

Like an antelope on the Serengeti Plain, Pesty was on the alert for any sign of danger. Hearing the irritation in my voice, she bolted from the room and made an unsuccessful attempt to disappear behind the umbrella stand in the foyer.

"Whatever it is that's going on between you two lovebirds, you'd better knock it off,

Charlie," warned Denny. "Your bride doesn't look like a happy camper. What's the matter, Jean? Anything ol' Den can do to help?"

Nettled by Charlie's endeavor to focus on my tobacco dependency, I narrowed my eyes and growled, "Yes, convince your friend 'Patch' that he has to wear a costume tonight."

"Don't waste your breath, good buddy," said Charlie. Taking hold of Denny's arm, he propelled the affable Scotsman out the back door. "See you later, bag lady."

Blessedly, my response was drowned out by the roaring motor of Denny's ancient MG convertible. Lighting a cigarette, I wondered how I was going to survive the night sans smoking.

Among the many changes made by Harrison Fowler at Sleepy Hollow was the ban on smoking in all areas of the club except the bar and grill. While the ban was generally well accepted, the same could not be said of the changes made in the club's menu.

Gone were many of the old favorites such as pizza, hot dogs, tacos, anything fried, and a host of calorie-laden desserts. The new fare was supposedly lighter and healthier. Upon finding the popcorn machine and the peanut dispenser replaced by canisters of unsalted pretzels and dried fruit, some disgruntled members began to disparagingly refer to the club as "Healthy Hollow." Harrison Fowler was not amused.

Deciding that I needed to reach out and touch someone, I picked up the phone and punched in my sister-in-law's familiar number.

"England's Fine Furniture. Happy Halloween. This is Mary. How may I help you?" The inquiring voice bubbled into the telephone.

"By having lunch with me today at the club." I tried to sound as upbeat as my friend and sister-in-law. "And if you can come up with something I can get that twin brother of yours to wear tonight, I'll give you a sneak preview of the dining room."

"You're on. It's been ages since we've had a chance to really talk, and I've got lots to tell you. Oh dear, gotta go. A customer just walked in. Pick me up at noon."

For the second time that morning, I was left holding the phone. "I don't know," I said to Pesty, who had returned from her self-imposed exile, "maybe it's me, but whatever happened to the old hello and goodbye?"

Seeing that I had nothing to offer in the

food department other than diet dog food, a disinterested Pesty crawled under the table and settled down for a nap. So much for companionship.

"You'd better watch it, my pretty," I warned in a menacing voice, "or I'll replace you with a ceramic kitty. At least I'd have its attention, and with no feeding or cleanup."

Dumping what was left of the morning's coffee down the drain, I loaded the dishwasher and wiped off the countertop before heading for the upstairs bathroom and a leisurely shower. If I was counting on the combination of hot water, shampoo, and body wash to jump-start my stalled creative juices, I would be sorely disappointed. My mind, like the rest of me (including my gray-streaked, auburn hair), had been washed clean.

No closer to resolving the costume problem than when I stepped into the shower, I shut off the water and wrapped myself in a thick, plum-colored bath sheet. The sheet, with its matching towels and bath mat, complement the white marble shower and tub surround. Rich, mahogany wood cabinetry with porcelain knobs introduce a measure of masculinity to the room, as does the wall arrangement of prints depicting various, well-known golf courses. A pair of brass hurricane lamps flank the large mahogany-framed mirror, which hangs over his and hers washbasins.

I stood in front of the vanity, waiting for the steam to dissipate. My thoughts drifted back to Harmon's curious visit to the club. That last conversation I'd had with him was as cloudy as the bathroom mirror. Perhaps with time, it too would become clear.

CHAPTER SEVEN

"Oh my stars, what a change. Just look at all the chrome and marble. And the color scheme, wow. White, black, and red with gold accents is so chic and elegant. If I didn't know better, I'd swear the walls were real marble and not faux. And the black-and-white ceramic tile floor is a classic. I feel as though it's the 1930s and I'm in the first-class dining room on the *Normandie* or the *Queen Mary.* The whole room just screams Art Disco."

I was about to correct her, but decided instead to chalk another one up for Mrs. Malaprop. "I'm glad you like the room," I said to Mary, giving her a hug.

"Like it?" squealed Mary, "why, I love it. And get a load of that chandelier. My stars, I've never seen one sparkle like that, especially in the daylight. It's absolutely beautiful. You sure didn't pick that baby up at some yard sale or flea market. It looks awfully expensive and like it was made for this room." Mary, who has exquisite taste, was right on all counts.

The chandelier was original to the room, but a combination of bad wiring and poor judgment resulted in its banishment until JR discovered it hidden in the club's storage room. I arranged for the piece, along with the entire dining room, to be rewired. Once the magnificent fixture was repaired and cleaned, it was returned to its rightful place in the center of the dining room's vaulted ceiling.

The heels of our shoes clicked, almost in unison, on the checkerboard pattern tile as we walked farther into the dining room.

"And just look at the windows. Look how the white linen panels with red-and-gold trim brighten up the place. What an improvement over those heavy, avocado monstrosities. And what a great idea to put a trio of King palms where the old bar used to be! Fabulous fake, by the way. And lighting them from below is a nice touch."

"Do you like it, Mar? Really, honestly like it?" I was concerned that family loyalty, coupled with our long and solid friendship, might have stripped my sister-in-law of objectivity.

Mary wrinkled her brow. "Are you kidding me, Gin?" she said, calling me by a best-be-forgotten childhood nickname. "The room looks absolutely, positively fabulous." Moving closer, she lowered her voice to a stage whisper. "But you know, my dear, for the sake of England's Fine Furniture, you must never, ever tell anyone where you got all this neat stuff. If you do, we'll lose all our customers to yard sales, salvage stores, and god forbid, those horrible flea markets."

Dramatically, she deposited her ample body in the nearest dining chair. "I know these chrome-and-leather dining sets aren't Gilbert Rohde. Not even Vanessa Higgins could afford them." Carefully lifting a corner of the snowy white tablecloth, she ran her hand over the tabletop and sides. "Truly, Gin, these are faithful reproductions. Where on earth did you find them? Don't tell me, let me guess. The Furniture Mart in Chicago. Am I right?"

I nodded my head. At the time of purchase, I had some concern regarding the sets. They were reproductions and priced higher than I'd originally planned on spending. Now, judging from Mary's positive reaction, I knew I had made the right decision.

"With you picking up marvelous bargains

all over the country, it's no wonder that poor Denny's losing his hair, mine's turned white almost over night, and England's Fine Furniture is going broke."

"Oh Mary, is the store really in trouble? Gosh, I'm so sorry. I just didn't have the funds this time around." I could feel a flush spreading across my face. "Harrison Fowler certainly wasn't any help, nor was Vanessa Higgins. I had to go where the bargains could be found or where I could use my discount."

Even though I spoke the truth, the explanation sounded lame; at least, it did to me. With the budget for the project being so tight, I hadn't ordered anything from England's Fine Furniture. Instead, except for the dining sets, I hunted for bargains at estate sales, salvage marts, and auction houses. When specific items such as white dinnerware with black-and-gold trim, tiered wall lamps, vintage posters, and distinctive statuary couldn't be found anywhere else, I'd dragged Mary to almost every flea market in central Indiana.

While I was busy doing my thing, JR was busy doing hers. She'd supervised the work being done by local subcontractors, coordinated schedules, followed up on promised deliveries, and managed to sweet-talk old man Wilson into removing all the trash left by the workers for practically nothing. My commitment to complete the challenging project on time and within budget was such that I'd virtually ignored everything else. This was something Charlie complained about on more than one occasion.

"My stars, Jean, what's happened to your sense of humor? I was only kidding. Of course it's not true, especially the part about the store being in trouble. Unfortunately, what I said about my hair and Denny's is all too true. I'm starting to look more and more like Martha Washington, but I blame it on inherited genes and not, as some have hinted, on my close association with De-signer Jeans."

Actually, Mary Hastings England is a very attractive woman. Like her twin brother, she has aged like a fine wine. My attempt to point this out was lost as Mary's attention shifted away from herself and back to the room and its contents.

"Oooh," she cried, popping out of the chair and rushing over to the huge ornate black-lacquered sideboard. "I love what you've done with this old thing. The ivory drawer handles are outstanding. Smuggled them out of Africa, I presume?"

It was more of a friendly accusation than

a question. Without waiting for a reply, Mary began fingering the silky, richly embroidered, fringed shawl that was casually draped across the cabinet's black granite top. A large, bronze sculptured elephant anchored the slippery fabric. The great sideboard, the vintage shawl, and the bronze sculpture worked beautifully together, creating a major focal point in the room.

Patting the elephant on its rump, Mary addressed the work of art as if it were a living thing. "Hey big fella, maybe you don't remember me but I sure remember you. I carried you across a parking lot that was so far from the main highway, I thought of sending postcards to the folks back home."

"Oh come now, Mary." I laughed. "It wasn't quite that bad or far. If I remember correctly, we both carried that elephant because it was so damn heavy. Besides, you're the one who insisted on parking there. You were terrified someone might recognize the England store logo on the side of your pickup truck."

"You're right about that. I didn't want anyone confusing England's Fine Furniture with Jean Hastings's flea market finds. But now that I see everything in place," said Mary, throwing open her short, plump arms as if to embrace the entire room, "it looks positively gorgeous. Even old Finky Dee could not have done better. God rest his soul," Mary added solemnly, "that is, if he had one."

To her credit, Mary had been a big help throughout the project — sometimes accompanying me on buying trips, sometimes babysitting Kerry and Kelly for JR. She is such an accommodating person, Charlie jokingly calls her the Third Jean.

Closing the dining room's new, frosted-glass double doors behind us, we headed down the west corridor leading to the bar and grill. I knew from Mary's critique of the room that it was a winner. Thanks to my friend, my confidence and sense of humor were renewed. I was finally ready to eat, drink, and listen to the latest gossip making the rounds in Seville.

CHAPTER EIGHT

We had barely gotten settled in the back booth of the grill when two glasses of water were unceremoniously plunked down on the tabletop. "You ready to order?" The question was posed by a young, attractive waitress who was obviously new to her profession and surroundings.

"Not hardly," I said. Since the table lacked menus, napkins, place settings, and an ashtray I dryly suggested that perhaps she'd forgotten something.

The girl was unflappable. "Oh yeah. I'm Tammie, and I'll be your server. Today's special is the veggie wrap and a cup of some kinda cream soup. Either broccoli or pea. It's kinda green. I think the two old duffers in the bar got the last of it, but I can check."

Pleased with her show of efficiency, which was still in its development stage, the young waitress leaned into the booth. "I better warn you," she said gravely, "Stella, the cook, is in a bad mood today because of all the fussing over tonight's big bash. Her and Mr. F. have been going at it all day. He keeps checking and double checking on everything and everybody. I'm almost sorry I was asked to work tonight."

Poor Stella. It was easy to imagine the pressure she was under having to prepare dinner for the expected crowd. I had advance knowledge of the menu thanks to my neighbor's son, Billy Birdwell. A full-time college student, the handsome kid was also working part-time as a waiter at the club. According to him, it was to be a sumptuous buffet with a choice of three entrees, salads, and vegetables. Great baskets of freshly baked rolls and sweet breads would also be available, along with a variety of imported cheeses, chilled fruit, and carafes of various Napa Valley wines. A portable bar was being set up at the far end of the room, next to the coffee and dessert carts. Mixed drinks, along with hors d'oeuvres, would be served tableside. In an effort to avoid confusion, seating at the tables would be prearranged by the club manager.

"We'll have two turkey clubs on white toast, hold the mayo on one and the lettuce on the other, two sides of slaw, and a small carafe of Webber's Bay Chardonnay. Put it all on my tab, Hastings, number 360."

"Cool," said Tammie, scribbling madly on a small order pad. "You know something, Mrs. H., if everyone ordered as good as you, this job wouldn't be so hard. Between you, me, and the wall, some people — I won't name names but her initials are V. H. — were a real pain in the ass today. Got all huffy when I told her that I'm a server not a slave. She sent her old man into the bar looking for the manager, Mr. Fowler, so he could bitch about me, I guess. But I'm not worried. Mac — you know, Tom MacNulty — was tending bar and he stuck up for me. That's what Billy told me. Mac's as nice as he's cute. Can you imagine that silly Lu-anne Stanford dumping him for that loser Gary Winslow? She's gotta be a little goofy, but with a mother like hers, I guess anybody could end up that way. You know of course, it's Luanne's mom, Mrs. Stanford who's really the boss of the whole shebang, includ-ing the car business."

Any further comments or revelations from Tammie were cut short by the appearance of Harrison Fowler. He acknowledged my presence with a slight nod of his head. After the disastrous meeting in his office, we'd reached an unspoken truce of sorts; I stayed away from him, and he avoided me. On the rare occasion when forced by circumstance to converse with me, the man was coldly polite.

Quickly switching gears, Tammie displayed a combination of discretion and efficiency that probably surprised even the girl herself.

"I'll get this in right away, ladies," Tammie said in a loud, pleasant voice, "and I'll be right back with some napkins and place settings." Spotting the cigarette case I'd taken from my purse, she added, "And an ashtray."

Flashing a smile in Harrison Fowler's direction, the girl rushed across the room and headed for the bar, stopping for a moment at the pass-through window to place our food order.

Tammie's timing was such that server, cook, and manager met with a resounding *thud* in the kitchen doorway. Our server managed to emerge from the three-way tangle virtually unscathed. She then fled to the bar area where, Mary and I assumed, she found safety and protection in the form of the bartender Tom MacNulty or "Mac" as she fondly called him. Harrison's reaction to the collision took place behind the now-closed kitchen door. If the cook and the manager were angry with the hapless Tammie, it was lost to our ears.

When the carafe of wine arrived, it was delivered by Mac, who informed us that Tammie, unlike Billy Birdwell, was not old enough to serve alcoholic beverages. Our server appeared a short time later, loaded down with the sandwiches, napkins, place settings, and an ashtray.

Arranging the various items on the table, Tammie let out an audible sigh. "Boy, oh boy. They sure screwed up when they didn't give the job of club manager to Mac. He knows way more about how to treat people than Mr F. First, he made sure I was okay, then he went right into the kitchen. Now, I don't know what he said to Stella or Mr. F., but when I went to pick up your order, the two of them were all nicey-nice to me and each other." Tammie's latest news bulletin was interrupted by the arrival of Cord and Winnie Stanford.

Owner of Stanford Motors, Seville's largest car dealership, and always the salesman, Cord waved a cheery, somewhat exaggerated hello. Winnie, his wife of some thirty years and a bit of a snob, busied herself with the menu.

When I was growing up, Cord Stanford's family lived down the street from mine, but that's about all the two families had in common. My parents, Tim and Annie Kelly, were members of the working middle class. Dad managed the local five-and-dime, and Mother taught piano. Cord's folks were successful lawyers, specializing in wills, trusts, and estates. The Stanfords had a full-sized grand piano, which nobody played. The Kellys owned a secondhand upright, which half the kids in the neighborhood pounded on at one time or another. While the Stanfords had more money, the Kellys had more fun and love. Lots and lots of love.

Cord, ten years my junior, never attended any of our local schools. Instead, his parents shipped him off to a series of East Coast boarding schools. By the time Cord had reached adulthood and returned to Seville, he was as much a stranger to his parents as he was to the rest of us.

Big, loud, and aggressive, Cord had made an unsuccessful foray into local politics before settling down as a luxury car salesman. His forceful personality was such that he somehow convinced Ray Carton, the elderly widower and owner of the dealership, to leave him everything. When Mr. Carton died a few months later, Cord had himself a successful business and an estate valued, at the time, at close to a quarter of a million dollars. A distant relative of Ray's attempted to overturn the old man's last will and testament, and eventually lost the battle in court.

As expected, the town gossips went wild, insinuating Cord might have had something to do with Ray Carton's death. Seeing that Ray, a heavy smoker, died from emphysema, it was more than a stretch to connect Cord Stanford with the event.

Shortly thereafter, Cord married Winnifred Crumm whose grandfather, Willie Crumm, was the infamous councilman of the ration coupon scandal that had rocked the town during World War II. For Winnie, the marriage was the stepping-stone she needed to regain some of the prestige her family lost because of Willie's shenanigans. The bride, like the groom, was politically, socially, and financially ambitious, making the union more a logical than a loving one.

Not wanting to risk the wrath of Harrison Fowler, Tammie announced to the Stanfords that she would be with them in a minute.

"Sorry ladies, I have to go. Enjoy your lunch, and if you need something more, give me a holler." Flipping her reddish-blonde braided hair over her shoulder, and with a tug on the too-tight uniform, the fresh-faced girl made a beeline for the Stanfords.

"Wanna bet that before our server is

through waiting on them, she'll have all the details on Luanne's divorce and her return to town with the baby?" Mary took a healthy bite of club sandwich, showering her ample bosom with toasted breadcrumbs. Like snowflakes in July, the debris didn't last long. With a swipe of her napkin, Mary quickly cleared the front of her blouse, scattering the toasty bits across the table.

"From what I hear, Mr. and Mrs. S. have been pushing the newly divorced Mrs. W. in the direction of your favorite club manager, Mr. F., and making Mr. M. one unhappy bartender."

"Jeez Mary, knock off the alphabet speak. Maybe Tammie can't help it but you certainly can. It's not like it's contagious — at least I hope it isn't. And please tell me that you've got something more interesting to talk about than yesterday's news," I said, extracting a broken toothpick from the wobbly stack of turkey, lettuce, tomato, and lean ham. At this point, the search for the missing portion of wood, not rehashed gossip, had my attention.

"Honestly," I grumbled, pulling the remainder of the toothpick from the pile of food on my plate, "I think we were better off with the old menu. Maybe all that stuff wasn't so healthy, but it wasn't deadly."

Holding the tiny, potentially lethal weapon between my finger and thumb, I gingerly deposited it in the ashtray.

Mary threw her hands up in disgust. "Are you about finished destroying your lunch? Would you care to start in on mine or would you rather we talk about what I came here to talk about? I thought maybe we could discuss a case of possible murder."

Knowing the effect the word *murder* would have on me, Mary immediately had my full attention. Any thought of food, healthy or otherwise, was forgotten. Pouring us both a second glass of the excellent chardonnay, I took a goodly sip and lit a cigarette.

"Really, Jean, you should quit smoking. Have you ever considered getting the patch? Believe me, it's a breeze with one of these. See?" Formerly a heavy smoker, Mary pulled up the sleeve of her brightly colored print silk blouse and proudly revealed a small, adhesive square stuck firmly on her fleshy, upper arm.

"See that," she said, pointing to the patch, "I haven't had a cigarette in almost two months. Fifty-one days, to be exact. It's wonderful how it controls my cravings. Trust me, the patch works. You can check it out with Doctor Parker. He's the one who suggested I give it a try. I think it's the same kind that he recommended to Charlie."

Exhaling, I blew the smoke from my cigarette away from Mary, sending a ghostly trail spiraling toward the whirling ceiling fan. "Yeah? Well, if it works so damn good, then why doesn't the good doctor use it himself? The man smokes like a chimney."

"He smokes cigars. Everyone knows that cigars aren't as bad for you as cigarettes," said Mary. "At least, that's what I've heard."

"Okay, great. I'll start smoking cigars. I'm sure your brother will love that. Now that my problem's been solved, maybe we can get back to the subject you were going to talk about. If I heard you right, it was something about a murder."

When I said the word *murder,* I'd raised my voice. For a moment, an uncomfortable silence engulfed the room. Then a nervous giggle escaped from Mary. It seemed to convince the other diners that the back booth was occupied by two women who couldn't hold their liquor. When the other customers returned to the business of minding their own business, a red-faced Mary proceeded to bring me up to date as to what had transpired at The Book Cellar in the days following Harmon's sudden death.

"In accordance with the law or Harmon's last wishes — I'm not sure which but whatever — there was this big, final, one-day-only sale. I thought for sure you'd be there. I guess you had too much to do, getting the room done and all. Anyway" — Mary paused to take another bite of her lunch before continuing — "with the furniture store being right next door to the bookstore and seeing how I wasn't able to attend the funeral, I felt it was the least I could do. If you're not going to eat your pickle, I'll take it."

Anticipating that the next request would be for my untouched coleslaw, I plunged the dill spear into it and passed the small crock to Mary. "Here, take the whole thing. I'm finished." If my impatience was showing, she ignored it. I waited while Mary polished off the pickle, slaw, and the last bite of her sandwich.

"Mmmm, that hit the spot. Now where was I? Oh yes, The Book Cellar's final sale. It was quite nice. You would've enjoyed it. Free gingersnaps and fruit punch. I don't know who furnished the refreshments. It might have been the lawyer. Or it could've been the college kids. Or maybe it was . . ."

"Mary, who the hell cares! Cut the crap and get to the point before I either run out of cigarettes or wine. In case you haven't noticed, I've already run out of patience."

"You know something, Gin, sometimes you can be so hard. I guess that's what makes you such a good sleuth."

"Okay, okay. So I'm a good sleuth, pay my taxes, and never fail to vote. Now tell me what does going to a book sale have to do with murder?"

"Well, when I was there, I kept thinking of Harmon and the horrible way he died. The more I thought of it, the more it didn't make sense. I can't believe that it happened the way they say it did." Mary adamantly shook her head, emphasizing her disbelief.

"No way would someone with a reputation for being overly cautious suddenly do something so careless. No way," Mary repeated. "Why, the man wouldn't even change a fuse without someone being there on the odd chance that he might get zapped. When the smoke alarms needed changing, he wouldn't touch them. Denny had to send Herbie Waddlemeyer over there to help him. Harmon was a nutcase when it came to personal safety. I don't believe he fell off that ladder. I think someone pushed him. That's what you think too, right, Gin?"

"Yeah," I said, "either that or someone pushed the ladder, causing Harmon to fall. Of course, thinking something is quite different from proving it. Here you have no witnesses, no weapon, no clues, and no motive." Lifting my glass of wine, I paused for effect before taking a drink, "Ergo, no case."

Mary was crestfallen. "I suppose you're right, seeing that you've had more experience with that sort of thing. I might as well throw this away," she said, waving the Halloween card she'd taken from her purse. "It probably wouldn't have been much help to you anyway."

The greeting card was the kind that you'd send to a small child. The witch depicted on the front of the card was more homey than homely and was holding a platter of pumpkin-shaped cookies. First I wondered if the wine had gotten to Mary, then I wondered if it had gotten to me. Try as I might, I could not connect the dots. "Okay, I give. How can a Halloween card help solve a mystery?"

"Now that's a silly question," said Mary. "It can't. The shame of it is, I was planning on sending it to Kerry and Kelly, but then I spoiled it by writing on the back. See."

Taking the card from Mary, I turned it over and scanned the list she had compiled.

NAME	GENRE
Dr. Parker	*fishing*
Chief Stevens	*true crime*

Tom MacNulty	*paranormal*
Jason Bowman	*chemistry*
Vanessa Higgins	*beauty*
Vern Higgins	*gardening*
Cord Stanford	*finance*
Harrison Fowler	*health*
Stella Robeson	*cooking*
Billy Birdwell	*science*

"Do you mind if I hang on to this?" I asked. "You never can tell about information. What seems unimportant now could end up being important later." I didn't have the slightest clue as to how Mary's little list related to Harmon's death, yet something told me to keep the card.

Mary's demeanor brightened considerably. "Of course you can keep it. After all, my whole purpose in making the list was to help you solve a mystery. Are you going to talk to Matt? Show him the list? I'll bet he thinks there's something fishy about Harmon's 'unfortunate accident,' too."

Actually, I had already discussed it with my son-in-law. He grudgingly acknowledged that there was something not quite right about Harmon's death. He also cautioned me that it wouldn't be in Designer Jeans's best interest if I were to become involved in another murder. He was referring to a little matter that had occurred the previous fall.

With his and JR's help, I was instrumental in solving the murder of Ida Sprigg, an elderly spinster. She'd met her death at the hands of a greedy nephew who held an antique, needlepoint pillow over her face. Matt made a big thing out of reminding me that Designer Jeans was a decorating firm, not a detective agency. I was to stick to my business and he would stick to his. It didn't help matters when Charlie supported everything Matt had to say on the subject.

Now only hours away from what could be Designer Jeans's biggest success, I was discussing another possible murder. Maybe the only unusual thing about the bookseller's death was the fact that it was so unexpected.

Instead of answering Mary's questions, I asked one of my own. "Are you about ready to go? If you see our elusive server before I do, flag her down. I'd like the check."

"Oh fudge," said Mary, "I was hoping to get us some dessert. It's such a nice way to end a meal."

"Forget it, Mar. I don't want it and you don't need it." I didn't mean to sound so callous. I should have apologized.

For the second time that day, my oldest and dearest friend accused me of being hard. Maybe she was right. I hoped not.

In an effort to make amends for unintentionally hurting her feelings, I gently reminded Mary that the bar and grill no longer offered such goodies as fried ice cream, pecan pie, double fudge cake, or ice cream sundaes topped with whipped cream, nuts, and cherries.

Mary wasn't disappointed. She was devastated. I had to do something to snap her out of it. It was time for tough love, or in this case, tough teasing.

"Now Mary, if you must have dessert," I said with mock sincerity, "you might consider ordering the fat-free frozen yogurt. It comes with trail mix and wheat germ sprinkles." It wasn't easy keeping a straight face while describing the bogus delicacy.

"Or perhaps," I added, aware of Mary's lifelong addiction to chocolate, "you'd prefer the chocolate tofu truffle sundae. After being frozen, the tofu is dipped in a mixture of rolled oats, cornmeal, and crushed bran flakes. Then the whole thing is covered in a cocoa prune whip and garnished with tiny pieces of dried figs."

"Okay, that's it." With a sharp slap to the flesh-colored patch on her arm, Mary exited the narrow booth like a cork shot from a bottle and loudly announced, "I'm outta here!" And she was.

At Mary's outburst, the errant Tammie came rushing over to our table. "Gee Mrs. H., I didn't realize you two were in such a big hurry. I'll get your check right away. I guess it's too late to tempt you ladies with our featured dessert. It's a pineapple-cheese glazed torte served with whipped cream. I had my doubts about you, but I thought for sure that the other lady would be interested. I guess I was wrong. Sorry."

Tammie wasn't the only one feeling wrong and sorry. I caught up with Mary in the foyer and was pleased to find that all was forgotten and forgiven. I didn't mention anything about tortes or toppings. I may be hard, but I'm not foolhardy.

CHAPTER NINE

I dropped Mary off at England's Fine Furniture and began the rather laborious drive home. Even though Seville has only five traffic lights, I managed to catch all of them. Turning onto Blueberry Street brought my minivan in direct conflict with small armies of trick-or-treaters, most of whom were more interested in what goodies they had accumulated than in practicing pedestrian safety. Few took the time to check traffic as they ran from house to house, crisscrossing the broad lawns and narrow streets. They carried their loot in plastic pumpkins or paper sacks. I even spotted one or two pillow cases.

"Saint Emeric," I prayed, recalling past Halloweens that were spoiled by careless or deranged adults, "please watch over the kids and keep them safe from harm."

Our town has taken steps to make Halloween safer by limiting the hours for trick-

or-treating. Parental supervision is encouraged as are school and church parties, and the hospital provides free x-rays of suspicious treats. Despite being aware of this, I couldn't shake the feeling growing inside of me that something was terribly wrong. It was as though I could reach out and touch the evil in the air.

Moments after my plea to the Irish patron saint of children, a figure dressed as the Prince of Darkness darted into the street. Because I was driving below the posted speed limit, I was able to stop the van in time. The almost victim appeared to be a male teenager.

"Hey asshole, watch where you're going," snarled the voice behind the mask. Reaching the safety of the sidewalk, he turned and gave me a parting middle-finger salute. I was beginning to have a real concern for my twin grandchildren's safety.

Shaken more from the near-miss than by the salute, I gladly traded the congestion of Blueberry Street for the less-populated, less-traveled Blueberry Lane. Surely, nothing untoward would pass this way, not even on Halloween.

A smattering of post–World War II houses dotted the lane. While most reflected the era's trendy ranch and split-level housing, number 707 Blueberry Lane did not. Modest in size and set back on an oversized lot, the house with its rough hewn siding and stone exterior, steep and gabled roof, and casement windows with muntins stood out from its neighbors.

The house was designed and built by Archibald Kettle, one of Seville's own. Kettle became a dedicated Anglophile as the result of residing in London during the infamous blitz. Having managed to survive the bombing of that city and the terrible war, Kettle returned to Seville, determined to re-create what he had come to respect and admire: the English country cottage.

When I was a kid growing up in in Seville, I loved the little house. I loved it even more when Charlie presented me with its keys on the day JR was born. Although we have lived in the house for more than three decades, everyone in town, including me, still refers to it as Kettle Cottage. I do so out of respect for Archibald Kettle. The townspeople do so purely out of habit, or as Charlie claims, out of pure Hoosier cussedness.

With the sky beginning to darken, the cottage looked more welcoming than ever. I could hardly wait to immerse myself in its safety and warmth. Making the turn onto the winding driveway, the van's temperamental wipers called it a day, leaving me to contend with a windshield covered in a thin layer of misty rain. On the ground, the dampness had turned the fallen leaves into great patches of mushy, decaying vegetation. Gone was the afternoon sunshine. The gentle caress of the soft breeze had been replaced by unexpected jabs of nasty, bone-chilling wind. The change in the weather brought a sudden end to the unusually warm and long Indian summer.

I parked the van on the asphalt apron and contemplated the short dash I had to make from vehicle to house. When I dropped Mary off after lunch, she'd given me a box marked "costumes," which she proclaimed were ready to wear. I tucked the large box under one arm, slung my purse over the other, and cautiously stepped out of the van and onto the wet, leaf-strewn pavement. Slip-sliding all the way, I breathed a sigh of relief upon reaching the back stoop of the cottage.

Opening the kitchen door, I was greeted enthusiastically by a committee of one. "And where, my pudgy pooch, is your master? Not out cleaning up leaves, that's for sure."

"You got that right." Charlie's voice floated out from the darkened living room.

The flaming candle inside of the carved pumpkin gave life to the traditional jack-o'-lantern face, casting an amber glow over the room and its contents.

"The master has been too damn busy handing out candy to half the kids in Indiana," the voice continued, "and he also donated the last of his pocket money to a group of teenagers collecting for some charity called 'Pizza for Peasants' or something like that. I wouldn't have had money for that except Denny thought he'd won all my dough so he skipped the bet on the last hole. Can you believe it? He beat me again."

Holding the nearly empty plastic bucket, Charlie entered the kitchen. "Look, we got about enough candy for a kid and a half. I hope you've got more stashed somewhere or we're going to have to start handing out dog biscuits or IOUs, neither of which would be particularly well received by the little monsters or their bigger counterparts. Boy, you should have seen the size of this one kid. He was really tall and dressed like the devil himself. He about scared the hell out of me. Even Pesty growled when she saw him. What a creep."

I was going to mention my own close encounter with the fallen angel but decided to let it go. Opening the pantry cabinet door, I reached for the extra package of peanut butter Kisses I'd hidden away. Refilling the bucket with a fresh supply of candy, I headed for the living room. Once my eyes adjusted to the candlelight, I spotted the small mountain of orange-and-black wrappers on the nearby end table. The cause of the temporary candy shortage at the Hastings was as plain as the nose on Charlie's face.

The grandfather clock in the hallway struck six, marking the end of trick-or-treating in Blueberry Lane. The scarcity of street lighting and sidewalks, coupled with an overabundance of mature trees and dense shrubbery, makes the lane a rather uninviting place once the sun drops behind the ridge that separates Seville from the country club. With less than an hour's time to shower and dress for the big event, I hurriedly opened the costume box.

I hoped Mary was right when she said they were ready to wear. I'd already decided that no matter what condition they were in, we were going to wear them. To my delight, everything needed was there and in tiptop shape. The outfits were so terrific, even Charlie liked them.

According to Mary, the costumes were given in lieu of paychecks to Will, the

England's eldest son, and his live-in girl-friend, Liz Becket. What had happened was that the off-Broadway production of *Everybody Goes to Rick's,* starring Will and Liz, folded suddenly due to some unresolved union problem. Before sailing for London, where they were to appear in a British revival of *Guys and Dolls,* the couple had shipped a large trunk full of their belongings, including the newly acquired costumes, to Mary and Denny for safekeeping.

According to Mary, Will and Liz had telephoned to say their goodbyes. When told of the club's dinner dance, Will suggested lending his favorite aunt and uncle the Ilsa and Rick costumes. He thought the outfits would be perfect for the occasion. Liz agreed, adding that in her opinion Charlie and I would look smashing as the ill-fated lovers.

I was surprised when Charlie offered no resistance once the 1940s-style tuxedo was out of the box. While the white jacket was a bit short in the sleeves, the rest of the outfit, including the shirt, bowtie, black trousers, and cummerbund fit fine. With his trim build, silver hair, and brooding eyes, Charlie made a superbly handsome Rick.

"Would you mind stepping out of the way so I can see if my seams are straight?" I asked, staggering over to the bedroom's mirrored closet doors. Somewhere between motherhood and menopause, I'd given up wearing shoes that raised my natural height to a level that would make half the players in the NBA drool with envy. "I've been on painting scaffolds lower and less wobbly than these strappy things. I don't think I'm cut out for this whole 'Ilsa' thing. I'm having second thoughts about this dress. It's so black and slinky, and the sequins are beginning to make me itch in places you wouldn't believe."

Moving closer to the mirror, I stared at my reflection. "Charlie, be honest. How's my makeup? Too much? And my hair, does it look funny in an upsweep? Should I ditch the earrings?"

Seeing that my husband had turned his back to me, I pushed myself away from the mirror. With one hand on my hip for dramatic effect and the other hand clutching the nearest bedpost for stability, I steeled myself for what was to come. Like Wyatt Earp entering the O.K. Corral, I was ready for a showdown. I proceeded to call the villain out.

"Charlie Hastings, you haven't heard a single word I've said. This time, chum, you're not getting away with it."

I was quick, but Charlie was quicker. "The dress is great, your makeup is just right, your hair never looked better, keep the earrings, and yes, I heard every word you said."

Turning around to face me, Charlie smiled as he handed me the oblong, white cardboard box. I was truly surprised. The last time I'd received something from Daisy's Garden Shoppe was on my birthday three years ago when Charlie presented me with six tomato plants and a bag of fertilizer.

"This is for you, sweetheart," said Charlie, "and be sure to read the card."

Nestled beneath the thin layers of green tissue paper was the biggest white orchid I'd ever seen. "Oh honey," I cried, lifting the huge flower from the box, "it's just beautiful. Help me pin it on my dress. Wait a sec, I've got to read the card first."

Thrusting the orchid into Charlie's outstretched hands, I pulled the small card from the folds of the tissue paper. The message was short, sweet, and in character: *Here's lookin' at you, kid. Love, Charlie.*

"How could you know that an orchid would be the perfect touch for my costume unless you knew in advance what I'd be wearing?" Then it hit me. "But you did know, didn't you. This proves that twins really do share a special bond. You two sure put one over on me. Just wait 'til I see Mary."

Pushing the florist pin through a small clump of spangle-encrusted material, Charlie managed to secure the beautiful flower to my dress. Taking a step back, he let out a low whistle of approval.

"You know something, kid, that fancy corsage is the perfect touch. Now you really look like a 1940s femme fatale. Come on, let's get out of here before I change my mind about wearing this monkey suit, twin or no twin."

A thick bundle of milky-gray fog pursued our small sedan as it slowly made the turn out of Blueberry Lane and onto the road leading to the country club.

"Hey sweetheart," said Charlie in a burst of unexpected enthusiasm, "even the weather is perfect. I feel like we're in the final scene from your favorite flick, *Casablanca.* What was it that Rick said to Louie?"

Expecting my usual recitation of the familiar film dialogue, Charlie was as surprised as I was when, in a raspy voice, I blurted out, "Something wicked this way comes."

CHAPTER TEN

"Holy smokes," Charlie yelped as he surveyed the club's dining room, "you and JR are more than good. You two are the absolute greatest. Everything looks so different. Bigger and better. Didn't I tell you that you were worrying about nothing? It's Art Deco updated. Wow!"

What further praise my husband might have had for the efforts of Designer Jeans was interrupted by a distinctive and friendly voice. "Hey Mrs. H., over here. It's me, Tammie."

"Oh good grief," Charlie said with dismay, "it's that scatterbrained waitress. She almost dumped the last of the cream of celery soup on me and Denny when we stopped in the bar for a quick lunch. (He would've been more dismayed had he known she'd referred to them as two old duffers.) It was quick, all right. She was so busy making goo-goo eyes at Mac and that kid from next door,

96

she tripped over her own two feet. You should have seen the mess she made. I swear, there was more soup on the bar than in our bowls."

At a podium positioned a few steps beyond the doorway stood Little Red Riding Hood, a.k.a. Tammie, the server. Dressed in a short, figure-hugging red dress with matching cape and hood, Little Red had never looked better.

"Gee, Mrs. H., I didn't know this guy belonged to you." She smiled broadly at Charlie. "Sorry about today, Mr. H. I'll tell you what, how about the next time you and your buddy order soup, it'll be on me." Laughing, she added, "Let's not tell Mr. F. He's liable to freak out. He's kinda fussy about the rules and stuff."

Tammie's words still hung in the air when Harrison Fowler entered the room and strode over to where the three of us were standing. He did not look happy.

"Tammie is supposed to inform people which table they've been assigned to. Is there a problem here? I hope not." Snatching the clipboard from the girl's hand, Harrison quickly ran his manicured finger down the neatly typed list of names. "Mr. and Mrs. Charles Hastings, table thirteen. It's the large, round one in the far corner."

Turning to Tammie, the manager gave her a withering look. "Now that wasn't so difficult, was it?" he snapped, not expecting an answer.

In an effort to defuse the situation, I made an attempt at flattery. "Why Harrison, you look absolutely perfect in your costume. It's a wonderful period piece and fits so well. You're the spitting image of Finky Dee." For Tammie's sake, I even managed to give him one of my best smiles.

Caught off guard by my friendly manner, the conceited jerk was momentarily at a loss for words and began removing nonexistent lint from the sleeves of his perfectly pressed black tuxedo. The clear polish on his manicured fingernails took on a pink glow, courtesy of the room's new lighting.

"What's that you say? I assume you're referring to Francis Dertz. I've heard the man was quite the cad and was given his just desserts in what is now my office. How unfortunate, I suppose, that his killer was never caught."

Shifting his attention away from us and out the nearby doorway where a growing number of automobiles waited for valet parking, Harrison smoothed his naturally wavy, color enhanced, black hair and straightened his already perfectly aligned bow tie. "If you'll excuse me, I have guests to greet."

With a final stern warning to mind the list, Harrison Fowler shoved the clipboard into Tammie's outstretched hands and headed for the foyer.

Tammie looked miserable. I thought she could do with a little moral support along with a verbal pat on the back.

"Come on, Tammie, don't let him get to you. Why, I think you're doing a great job. So does Mr. Hastings. Tell her, Charlie."

"What? Oh yeah, sure. Hey, nobody serves soup the way you do, Red." Charlie grinned when he added, "and honey, I've got the stains to prove it."

Tammie responded to Charlie's charm by planting a big kiss on his cheek. "Like I was sayin' before we was interrupted, the next time the soup's on me, but don't order the corn chowder. I don't look so hot in yellow."

I waited until their shared laughter subsided before asking Tammie if she could tell me who else had been assigned to table thirteen. She assured me that it wouldn't take more than a minute or two. Wrong. It took forever, or so it seemed. I was about to tell her to forget it when she looked up from the clipboard and blinked her pale eyes.

"You understand, Mrs. H., I can't go making changes. If I did, you-know-who would kill me. Now let's see. First, there's you and Mr. H. Then there's Vernon and Vanessa Higgins, the ass and the pain, if you get my drift." Tammie snickered, making no effort to keep her voice down. Clearly, Harrison's attempt at employee intimidation had failed.

"Shoot, Mrs. H., if that weren't bad enough, you guys got stuck with Mr. F. and his date. Wanna bet it's the gay divorcee, Luanne Winslow? Oh, and then there's a Bowman, J. No way of telling if it's a him or a her. Sorry."

Hugging the clipboard to her chest, Tammie frowned. "There was one other person for table thirteen, but I can't read the name. It's been all crossed out with one of those markers. I guess whoever it was must've like canceled or something."

"Or, like, died," I mumbled. Since the seating had been worked out well in advance, it was more than likely that it was Harmon Brinker's name beneath the heavy ink.

"I heard that, Jean. This is supposed to be your big night. Remember?" said Charlie. He was peeved. "We're here to eat, drink, and have fun, period. We are not here to discuss the dead be they past, present, or future."

With a tight grip on my arm, Charlie all but dragged me across the room to table thirteen, where I was deposited in the nearest chair. We were the first of the table's occupants to arrive. After ordering me to stay put and out of trouble, Charlie announced that he was going to the west wing's bar and grill for a drink, even if it was only water.

It was my pleasure to inform him that the entire west wing was closed for the night. "Sorry dear, I guess you'll have to wait for the tableside drink service to begin, and that's not going to happen until everyone's been seated."

Charlie took the news badly. "For chrissakes, who the hell knows how long that's going to take? Meanwhile, I could die of thirst. The roof of my mouth feels funny, my tongue's all rough, and my throat's dry. I probably caught some kind of virus. What do you think, sweetheart?"

"I think someone ate too many peanut butter Kisses, that's what I think. That'll do it every time. Try to hang in there, chum. The place is starting to fill up fast."

What I'd said was true. The trickle of guests coming through the doorway had increased to flood proportions.

"Look," I cried, waving at a small knot of people threading their way across the room, "there's JR and Matt with Mary and Denny. It's kind of hard to tell with the costumes and all, but I think the Stanfords are right behind them. Jeez, half the town seems to be headed this way!"

Because I was standing, I had an almost-unobstructed view of the entire room. I had finally gotten the hang of maneuvering in the platform shoes with the spikey heels and no longer needed help moving about. The footwear was reasonably comfortable, and made my legs look better than they had in years.

"Chief Stevens is here," I said. "How nice. This time he remembered to bring his wife and leave the cat at home. Hey, I see the Parkers. At least, I think it's the Parkers. From the size of this crowd, I'd say the gang's all here and then some."

"Let me know when you spot the ass and the pain, if you get my drift," said Charlie, borrowing words from his new favorite waitress. "The sooner they get here, the sooner I can get something to quench this awful thirst. And for your information, Jean, I only ate a couple pieces of that candy. Three or four at the most."

We were in the midst of arguing the effects of pigging out on peanut butter Kisses versus the odds of contracting jungle fever in the heart of popcorn country when Mr. and Mrs. Higgins made their entrance. It was a real kicker, as they say in this neck of the woods.

His bald head, rotund body, and doleful expression made Vernon Higgins the perfect Canio, the heartbroken and jealous clown whose tragic story is told in Leoncavallo's *Pagliacci*. The ruffled, black-and-white satin costume looked like it'd been plucked from La Scala's wardrobe department. Stark white grease paint covered his face. Someone, most likely Vanessa, had drawn the traditional teardrop on his droopy right cheek.

"While I know who he's supposed to be, I'm not too sure about her. Maybe the unfaithful Nedda?" Like everyone else, I was staring at Vanessa Higgins. "What's your guess, Charlie?"

"I don't have one," he said as we watched the May/December couple work the crowd like a pair of seasoned politicians. "If I did, I'd guess she's a frustrated hooker who's looking for business in all the wrong places. Somebody ought to tell her to go home and put on some clothes."

Vanessa's long, platinum blonde hair was hanging loose and free. Her makeup was perfect as always, although she did appear to be wearing more than her usual amount of eyeliner, shadow, and mascara. Attired in an extremely low-cut black-satin-and-lace peignoir set, she was positively X-rated.

It was only after Vernon Higgins plopped the pointy, broad-rimmed black satin hat on his wife's head that the truth of the matter dawned on me. "Oh good grief, she's a witch!"

"Ain't that the truth, dearie." The almost lighter than air, purple plumage sticking out of JR's elaborate Gibson Girl hairdo bobbed in agreement. Until she spoke up, I wasn't aware that JR and her group had moved within hearing distance.

Dolled up as a Gay Nineties dance-hall queen, JR looked adorable. The taupe-colored taffeta gown emphasized her slim figure and brought out the tiny flecks of gold in her eyes.

Matt was decked out as a riverboat gambler of the same era. He looked tall, dark, and handsome in the frilly, white shirt, black pants and vest, snakeskin cowboy boots, and a fake mustache. He was also toting a toy derringer.

The Englands came in costumes that

reflected their patriotism. Denny wore a medal-festooned doughboy uniform from World War I. Mary's uniform was a white two-piece sailor suit. The bell bottom trousers fit her perfectly, and the oversized blouse flattered her figure.

Doctor and Mrs. Parker were wearing identical green hospital scrubs. Their outfits included surgical booties, gloves, caps, and masks. Covered up as they were from head to toe, the senior-citizen couple might have pulled off their little charade of being twins had it not been for the doctor's wolf whistle approval of Vanessa's eye-popping costume. The whistle removed all doubt as to which one was the doctor and which one was the wife. For his misstep, Doctor Parker received a swift kick in the shins delivered with gusto by Mrs. Parker.

The Parkers, along with the Englands and the Cusaks, had been assigned to table twelve.

All eyes were upon her as Vanessa purposely wiggled her way to table thirteen. With everyone watching the blatant display of sensuality, no one noticed the arrival of Harrison Fowler and his date, Luanne Winslow. Although she wore a French maid uniform, the young divorcee looked more wholesome than sexy.

Luanne's protective father and her pushy mother had already been seated at table fourteen along with Chief Stevens and his wife. Claiming it was a coincidence, Winnie Stanford and Martha Stevens were dressed alike in flapper outfits that matched right down to the beaded headbands, rolled-to-the-knees hosiery, and feather boas. In keeping with the Roaring Twenties theme, Cord Stanford and Rollie Stevens each sported a raccoon coat, porkpie hat, and carried a Sev-Vale College pennant. Some coincidence.

"Vernon, honey, be a darlin' and see if y'all can get Mac's attention," drawled Vanessa, languidly sliding into the empty chair to the right of Harrison Fowler. Luanne, seated to the club manager's left, stiffened visibly at the mention of the bartender's name.

"Let him know that y'all need some drinks here. Ah do declare, sometimes that man's service is as bad as his manners. Y'all know what Ah'm sayin'?"

If looks could kill, Vanessa would have been dead and Luanne charged with her murder.

The moment passed, seemingly forgotten, by the time Billy Birdwell came bouncing up to our table.

"Good evening, folks. Happy Halloween and welcome to the reopening of Sleepy Hollow's main dining room. Would anyone care to order a drink?" In less time than it took to ask the question, it was answered.

"All right," said Billy turning to Vanessa, "I'll start with you Mrs. Higgins. What would you like?"

"Ah do declare, silly Billy, y'all ready know what Ah like. Y'all know what Ah'm sayin'?"

The young waiter handled the double-entendre with a maturity that belied his age. Tapping himself lightly on the head to indicate that he had forgotten something, Billy turned away from Vanessa and directed his reply to her husband.

"Please excuse the lapse in my manners, Mr. Higgins. I should have approached you first and allowed you to order for the lady. Let me assure you sir, it won't happen again."

Vernon Higgins, a member of the old school, accepted Billy's apology and went on to order drinks for himself and his wife. Harrison and Charlie had the good sense to follow suit. This method of ordering was rather archaic; nevertheless, it got the job done without any further disruptions.

The drink order ended up to be a fairly simple one: three lite beers and three spicy

Bloody Marys. The amiable Billy then suggested changing the order from six individual drinks to a party-size pitcher of lite beer and a party-size pitcher of Bloody Marys. This would enable everyone to have a second drink without the wait and the pitchers would be easy to refill. Everyone liked the two-pitcher suggestion, especially the part about eliminating the delay. Charlie wasn't the only one at the table who was in desperate need of a drink.

"Great," said Billy, "I'll be right back with your order and some frosted mugs for the beer drinkers. Those of you having Blood Marys are in for a real treat. The glasses will be rimmed with Mac's special, secret seasonings."

Stepping back from the table, the solidly built waiter collided soundly with Jason Bowman, almost knocking the scrawny chemist to the floor.

"Gosh, Mr. Bowman," said an embarrassed Billy, "I didn't see you standing there. I'm awfully sorry, sir."

"No problem," Jason replied quietly, "it was more my fault than yours. The nice young lady in the red cape informed me that I was to sit with these good folks."

When Jason joined us, the seating arrangement at the table, starting from the top and going clockwise, was as follows: Harrison Fowler, Luanne Winslow, Charlie, me, Jason Bowman, Vernon Higgins, and last, but certainly not least, Vanessa Higgins.

Jason was wearing a single-breasted black suit, white shirt, and a western-style string tie. The middle-aged, soft-spoken man looked more like an itinerant country preacher than one of Valley Lab's brightest and most valued employees.

Painfully shy, he explained in a halting voice the reason for his late arrival and for not being in costume. "I, um, stopped to visit Mother and Harmon. Their plots practically adjoin, you know. I guess, I, um, lost track of the time. I find it hard to believe that they're, um, both gone now, especially Harmon. Don't you?" With sad, owl-like eyes, Jason looked around the table. An uneasy silence followed.

"Yo, Bowman," said Charlie, attempting to steer the conversation in a different, lighter direction, "how are things down at the lab? Rumor has it that you're working on something really big, like Valley's version of the pill for guys. It supposedly has saved more marriages than Doctor Ruth."

Jason blushed and coughed delicately. "Oh no, certainly not. What I'm working on will be a benefit to people of all ages, regardless of gender. It might even, um, you know, save some lives as well. At least, I, um, hope it will."

Uncomfortable with being the center of attention, Jason sought help from Vernon Higgins. "Even though he's retired from the day-to-day business of running Valley Labs, I'm sure Mr. Higgins would be more than happy to talk shop, so to speak."

Leaning back in his chair, Vernon Higgins folded his short, stubby arms over his considerable belly and cleared his throat.

"Why I'd be glad to. Sorry to say, I haven't the vaguest idea what Bowman here is working on, although I'll admit that the competition hit the jackpot with their little pill. I also have to admit that since I've been taking it, my performance in the bedroom has vastly improved. It has made a big difference in our marriage. Ask Vanessa. She can tell you."

The saying "there's no fool like an old fool" certainly applied to Vernon Higgins.

Unlike her husband, Vanessa was speechless. The color had drained from her beautiful face, and her breathing seemed to have stopped. When she lowered her head, I thought for sure she was going to faint but I was wrong.

Witnessing her public humiliation, I

silently wondered if Vanessa had knowingly traded self-respect for a life of wealth and privilege. Then, as if she'd read my mind, Vanessa raised her head, and her cold, blue eyes met mine. I knew the answer. It was an unequivocal yes.

We were spared any further revelations pertaining to the sexual aspects of the Higgins marriage by the timely return of Billy Birdwell pushing a trolley of drinks.

"Oh, thank god," Charlie whispered in my ear, "my prayers have been answered."

"Well goody for you," I whispered back, "mine haven't. I still can't smoke in here."

CHAPTER ELEVEN

"Pardon me. If it's okay with everyone, I'll go ahead and put everything, including this selection of Stella's delicious appetizers, in the center of the table."

When no one objected, the young waiter set about transferring most of the trolley's contents to the middle of the table. The minute this was accomplished, the table erupted in a flurry of activity.

Glasses, mugs, and pitchers were moved about as Stella's wonderful hors d'eouvres made their way from platter to plate to mouth. Jason Bowman asked for, and received, a chilled bottle of mountain spring water. Luanne, Vernon, and Charlie were the beer drinkers, leaving the pitcher of Bloody Marys for me, Vanessa, and Harrison Fowler.

Tipping one of the frosted mugs ever so slightly, Charlie filled it to the top with the golden, foamy brew. He then presented the mug to Luanne. "This one's for you, my pretty maid," he said, roguishly twirling an imaginary mustache.

Under the spell of Charlie's charm, Luanne bloomed. "All for me? How can I ever thank you, kind sir? There must be something I can do for you. Does anything come to mind, or would you like to think about it for a while? I can wait if you can."

Luanne's coquettish response, which included a provocative wink and smile, added to the humor of the interplay. Enjoying her part in the frivolity, the petite divorcee with the dark hair and even darker eyes, seemed unaware of her mother's attempt to eavesdrop on the flirtatious conversation.

The eldest of Winnie and Cord Stanford's five daughters, Luanne was the prettiest and smartest of the bunch. She shocked everyone in town when she broke off a three-year relationship with Tom MacNulty and eloped with Gary Winslow, Sleepy Hollow's former golf instructor.

A scratch golfer, Gary believed he had what it takes to turn pro. The ability was there but not the discipline or the dedication. Luanne accepted her husband's shortcomings until they included gambling and infidelity. They were living hand to mouth in Vegas when he left her for an exotic dancer.

Luanne's mother refused to accept the fact that the marriage, which she'd championed, had failed. Winnie continued to refer to Gary as her son-in-law, the pro golfer. She glossed over his absence with the explanation that he'd joined the PGA tour.

Seville's gossips feasted on the whole sordid mess. Most of the talk centered around whether or not Luanne and Mac could rekindle the flame of their once-red-hot romance. The question would remain unanswered until Mac and Luanne were ready to go public with their private feelings. Judging from Luanne's reaction to Vanessa's stinging criticism of Mac, it was obvious to everyone at table thirteen that the spark was still there.

Ignoring the rattle of ice cubes coming from the glass that Vanessa was holding, I slowly poured myself a drink and deliberately returned the heavy, glass pitcher to the center of the table. It was my way of showing the narcissistic Mrs. Higgins that I was neither her server nor her slave.

One forlorn look from Vanessa brought three men to her rescue: Vernon, Jason, and Harrison. They practically arm wrestled one another for possession of the pitcher. Vernon was a surprise. For an old guy, he was pretty quick, almost as quick as Jason. Alas, in the end, the milquetoast chemist proved to be no match for the agressive club manager.

"See here, Bowman, I'll take it if you don't mind. The lady and I are sharing."

It crossed my mind that perhaps a pitcher of Bloody Marys wasn't the only thing the two were sharing.

Vanessa's helpless act rankled me. It was bogus, like the woman herself. This was someone who, not that long ago, was balancing trays of overfilled drinks and cups of scalding coffee while propelling a cart the size of a small, armored tank, down the narrow aisle of a commercial jet. And now she couldn't hoist a pitcher of vodka and tomato juice? I needed a break from the witch in the naughty nightie. I also needed a cigarette.

Planning to slip quietly out of the dining room, I gathered up my purse and drink. I gently pushed my chair away from the table at the same moment that Harrison Fowler, drink in hand, suddenly stood up.

"Oh brother," I mumbled under my breath, "it figures. I decide it's time for a smoke and Mr. Toastmaster decides its time for a speech. He'll probably talk for hours."

Reluctantly, I moved my chair back to its original position. Having been raised by a mother who ranked Emily Post second only to Eleanor Roosevelt in wisdom, grace, and deportment, I hadn't any choice other than to sit there and give the club manager my full and undivided attention.

Charlie inched his chair closer to mine and said in a low voice, "Did you know that you were muttering again? You always do that when you're out of sorts. If you were wearing the patch, you wouldn't be so grumpy."

Setting down an almost full mug of beer, he took my hand in his and gave it a squeeze. "Hey kid, you know I love you whether you smoke or not. I wish you would at least try the patch. If not for me, then do it for Kerry and Kelly."

"How dare you drag the grandchildren into this." My husband was starting to aggravate me almost as much as a certain former flight attendant. "Would you like to know what I wish, Charlie? I wish the hell you'd stop talking about that damn patch. If not for me then do it for Pesty."

Unable to determine whether or not I had verbally scored a hit, I decided to reload and try again.

"Charlie, dear, what do you think really

happened to Harmon when he was on that ladder? Mary insists he was murdered. She practically begged me to take on the investigation." Bingo!

Pleased with the effect this had on my husband (his face went from tan to white to red), I then chug-a-lugged the Bloody Mary cocktail. The savory seasonings that rimmed the glass mixed with the potent potable, creating a surprisingly different and delightful taste. It also brightened my mood.

Taking a moment to assess the situation, Charlie proposed a truce, which I readily accepted. We were exchanging heartfelt apologies when an irritating shushing sound went around the table. The club manager, so it seemed, was about to begin his speech.

Swaying slightly, Harrison appeared to be having trouble clearing his throat. His left hand moved frantically to the breast pocket of his tuxedo, where a triangle of white handkerchief peeped out. In his right hand was a cocktail glass, its contents untouched. The guttural sounds coming from him were disturbing. Only Vanessa was crass enough to comment.

"Harrison, would y'all *please* stop makin' that awful noise. It's disgustin'. Y'all know what Ah'm sayin'?"

As if he were obeying her command, the

onerous club manager fell silent. The rimmed glass slid through his fingers, spilling vodka and tomato juice before coming to rest on the tabletop. Harrison quickly followed suit. The dark, red liquid on the white tablecloth formed a bloodlike halo around his head.

Suspended animation was the term I would use when asked later to describe my immediate reaction to Harrison's collapse. It felt as though something wicked had decended upon the dining room and sucked the life force out of everybody and everything.

This morbid state of inertia ended when Doctor Parker, looking grimmer than usual, announced solemnly, "I'm afraid there's nothing I can do for him now. The man is dead." The doctor was referring to the club manager, Harrison Fowler, who indeed was a dead man.

The wave of applause started at table fourteen and began with Chief Stevens. It quickly spread over the dining room. The only people not joining in the ovation were those seated at tables twelve and thirteen.

Believing the death to be staged and part of the evening's entertainment — a make-believe murder with everyone participating in its solution — the people stopped clap-

118

ping and quieted down, eager for the play and players to continue. And that is exactly what they thought was happening when Stella, the cook, screamed and dropped a huge platter of thinly sliced roast beef au jus. The crowd responded with a fresh round of applause and Stella responded by making a mad dash for table thirteen.

Her white chef's apron was spattered with bloody juices, thanks to the dumped meat. Droplets of the stuff managed to find their way to her sweaty face and frizzy brown hair. A small sob escaped from her as she draped herself protectively over the body of the club manager. Doctor Parker attempted to intervene, but when he touched her, Stella became hysterical. Shrieking and moaning, she rolled from the table and slipped to the floor where she lost consciousness.

Anxious to stave off any further ovations and to take control of the situation, Matt Cusak moved quickly to the center of the room. In or out of uniform, the tall, no-nonsense law officer exudes authority.

The product of a failed teenaged marriage, Matt grew up in a series of foster homes. He learned about life on the mean streets of St. Louis. At seventeen, he joined the Marine Corps. After four years of military service, followed by a year spent mostly enjoying the beaches of sunny Florida, Matthew K. Cusak migrated back to the Midwest. He more or less drifted from city to city, and job to job, before landing a part-time position as a police dispatcher in Bard's Valley, a small suburb located to the south of Indianapolis.

Eager to make law enforcement his life's work, Matt took as many courses as he could at various local junior colleges. Eventually, he transferred to Indiana University where he met JR. Shortly after graduation, the two married and settled in Seville, where Matt was offered a permanent position with the Seville Police Department.

Twelve years and almost as many promotions, pay raises, and promises later Matt, along with the town council, was still waiting for Chief Rollie Stevens to retire. Although this was something that was long overdue, the eccentric Rollie had an ironclad contract with the town, making it virtually impossible to force him out until he was damn good and ready to go.

"Quiet, please," Matt said in a loud, clear voice that carried as far as the foyer and beyond. "I'd appreciate it if you would remain seated until I'm done speaking. This is not a game. What has happened here is not part of any kind of entertainment."

A surge of astonishment passed through the crowd. Some people gasped while others voiced their disbelief. What Matt had told them couldn't possible be true. Or could it?

"Chief Stevens asks that you vacate the premises immediately and in an orderly fashion," Matt went on to say. "Only those seated at tables twelve, thirteen, and fourteen, Billy Birdwell, and Tom MacNulty are being asked to remain. The rest of you are free to go. Please do so, now."

In deferring to the chief, Matt was going by the book. He was also covering for a fellow officer and former Marine. Rollie Stevens had committed a major faux pas when he led the applause for the club manager's deadly performance.

With his brown skin, full red lips, raisin-like eyes, and closely cropped, silver hair, Rollie Stevens looked more like a big, gingerbread cookie than our town's top law officer. Clutching the college pennant, he slowly waved it at Matt as if he were sitting in the bleachers waiting for the big game to begin. In retrospect, it already had.

CHAPTER TWELVE

The conga line of departing autos in the foggy parking lot temporarily came to a halt, making way for the arriving police and emergency vehicles. As uniformed personnel entered the club, all those who had been asked to stay, except for Chief Stevens and Doctor Parker, were herded down to the west wing's bar and grill by Officer Patti Crump.

New to the force, the former heavy equipment operator was moonlighting that night as a car jockey. Upon learning a death had occurred, Patti immediately removed the valet parking sign from the clubhouse's portecochere and reported for duty.

"Lieutenant Cusak wants everybody to stay put," she barked. "That means no sneakin' off to the kitchen or john. He says he'll be down to talk to you people ASAP. He don't want nobody duckin' out, and I'm gonna stay in that there hallway, makin' sure that don't happen." Having said this, the amazonian Patti turned on her heel and took up her post in the west corridor.

Our internment in the bar and grill was rather pleasant under the circumstances. Mac, with help from Billy, managed to set out an impromptu spread of pretzels, celery, stuffed olives, chocolate mints, and pots of hot tea and coffee. The ingenious duo scrounged up a small supply of foam cups, plastic stirrers, and cocktail napkins. The end result was far from grand (the word *pathetic* comes to mind), but everyone appreciated it with one exeception: Vanessa Higgins, which surprised no one.

While Vernon and Vanessa sat in stony silence at a table for two, the Stanfords, Lucy Parker (the doctor's wife), and Martha Stevens (the chief's wife), took refuge in the middle booth. Their conversation was polite if somewhat strained. Luanne, Mac, Jason, and Billy were in the bar watching a televised Halloween special. Charlie and I shared pretzels, mints, and hot tea with Mary, Denny, and JR in the grill's oversized back booth. We passed the time away swapping legendary folktales and the like.

Mary was about to tell the story of Great-Uncle Fortesque Hastings and the Murphy bed when the ambulance transporting the heavily sedated Stella Robeson pulled out of the parking lot. With its siren blaring and lights whirling, it was obvious the vehicle was on an emergency run with no time to waste.

For the occupants of the bar and grill, the opposite was true. We had time to waste, time to spare, and time on our hands. And one of us even had time to kill.

The light mood we'd been enjoying was beginning to crumble. Seeking to restore it, I turned to the one person who I knew could handle the job.

"Say Mar, wasn't it Uncle Fortesque who sued his wife for divorce on the grounds that she spent the money faster than he could make it. Instead of getting the divorce, he got ten to twenty years for counterfeiting."

"Oh my stars," said Mary, purposely dropping a chocolate mint in her cup of hot tea, "you've got the wrong man."

"Yeah, that's what he said, but they tossed him in jail anyway," quipped Charlie, knowing his remark would get a laugh.

Mary briskly stirred her tea. Unintentionally funny, the self-appointed family historian waited for the laughter to die down before setting the record straight.

"It was Forsyth, not Fortesque, who ran

afoul of the law. They were identical twins, which is probably why you mixed them up. People were always doing that. I don't know why. They had such different personalities. Forsyth was very artistic. The Secret Service called his C-note a masterpiece. Fortesque was the scientific one. In 1925, the federal government credited him with the development of the first microbrewery."

She paused to catch her breath and to drink some of the sweetened tea. Once this was done, Mary was ready to continue.

"Now that I've unmixed the twins, perhaps I can tell the story of Fortesque and the Murphy bed with a mind of its own. Uncle swore that the thing was possessed."

She had gotten to the part where Uncle Fortesque hired a mail-order preacher to exorcise the bed when a slow-moving vehicle crept by the grill's long bank of windows. It was the ambulance carrying Harrison Fowler's corpse. Out of respect for the dead, we bowed our heads and observed a moment of silence. The moment passed and so had the ambulance. It seemed to have simply disappeared, "just like that preacher fella and Uncle's fiancee did when he caught the two of them buck naked in the Murphy bed," said Mary, determined to finish the story.

"According to Fortesque, the demon bed first folded itself into the wall with the fornicators trapped inside. Then, it it slowly came down again, but this time the bed was empty! Poor old Forty was convinced the whole episode was a true, paranormal experience until the two lovebirds were arrested in a Wal-Mart store somewhere in Idaho. They were trying to cash one of Uncle's social security checks."

Mary unwrapped a chocolate mint and popped it in her mouth. "You know, when you think about it, that's an awfully long way to go just to cash a check, especially when you're not wearing any clothes."

Her comment, like her story, triggered unbridled laughter. While such boisterous and demonstrative behavior might not have been proper, given the reason for our being there, it helped relieve the tension. By the time Matt was ready to talk to us, the occupants of the back booth were relaxed and ready to hear what he had to say.

Flanked by Chief Stevens on one side and Doctor Parker on the other, Matt signaled to Patti Crump, who lost no time turning off the television and escorting Luanne, Jason, Mac, and Billy to the grill's nearest vacant booth.

When everyone was seated, Matt explained the situation. Doctor Parker wasn't able to determine the exact cause of Harrison Fowler's death. The body was being transported to the morgue where Dr. Sue Lin Loo, the county medical examiner and pathologist, would perform the autopsy. Since foul play could not be immediately ruled out, Matt would need a statement from each one of us.

"Any questions?" he asked rhetorically, taking special care not to make eye contact with me.

Like a phoenix rising from the ashes, Vanessa Higgins was on her feet. "Ah don't know about the rest of y'all, but Ah've just about had it with these Keystone Kops. Come on, Vernon honey, we're goin' home." Turning around, she literally and figuratively, found herself up against an immovable Patti Crump.

"Sit down, lady," Patti growled at the startled Vanessa. "Nobody leaves 'til Chief Stevens says so. Ain't that right, Lieutenant?" Along with the rest of the police force, the rookie cop knew which man really ran the show. She also knew that Matt expected every officer to treat the elderly chief with the utmost respect.

"Well Ah never!" shouted Vanessa. Her heaving breasts threatened to escape from the loose confines of her satin nightgown. "Ah never did see such a fuss bein' made over nothin' in all ma born days. Rollie Stevens, if ya'll had half a brain instead of an empty head, ya'll would fire the whole bunch, startin' with that he-she Patti Crump and endin' with that lummox of a lieutenant. Y'all know what Ah'm sayin'?"

Expecting JR to erupt in a fury, I looked to Charlie for help. In a move designed to restrain rather than to protect, he wrapped his arms around JR. Unable to free herself, she could only watch as Martha Stevens, the chief's wife, sprang into action.

The grandmotherly woman marched across the room, coming to a halt within inches of Vanessa's face. "Young woman, you shut that big mouth of yours or I'll shut it for you. My husband doesn't need a gussied-up tart telling him how to run the police department. Everybody in this town knows that Patti Crump is a better person than you could ever hope to be, and Matt Cusak is the best thing that ever happened to the force."

For a minute, everyone in the grill thought that the tiny Martha was going to deck the witchy Mrs. Higgins.

Martha's scathing words were still being digested by a shocked Vanessa when Sergeant Sid Rosen hustled the feisty, Cuban-born Martha Stevens into the bar, where he could meticulously record her statement. What remained of the evening became an arduous waiting game. Martha's statement was the first to be taken. Mine was the last.

CHAPTER THIRTEEN

"Well Mr. Know-It-All, you're right again," I said to Charlie the next morning as I filled his plate with a second helping of bacon, scrambled eggs, hash brown potatoes, and buttered sourdough toast.

Too tired to eat when we finally arrived home the night before, we were making up for it with a hearty country breakfast. This was something greatly appreciated by Pesty. With her usual speed, she devoured everything in her dog dish. The bowl had been licked clean of Dandy Diet Dog Chow and a small helping of people food. Satisfied for the time being, Pesty sat down as close to my chair as possible without actually being in it. This unusual display of camaraderie was her way of thanking me for the extra rations.

"Of course I am," said Charlie between sips of freshly squeezed orange juice. "Now would you care to fill me in on the details?"

With my mouth full of breakfast, it was easier for me to show rather than tell. Placing a copy of the *Seville Sentinel,* our town's daily newspaper, on the table, I used my fork as a pointer. In doing so, a small blob of scrambled egg landed on the headline.

" 'Man Dies at Diner,' " Charlie read aloud. "Say, I'll bet it was the hash that did him in. Remember how sick I got last time I ate at Max's? I swear it was the hash."

Taking a napkin, I removed the morsel of food. "Don't be a dolt. Read it again, chum. It reads, 'Man Dies at Dinner.' So you're right. The grand reopening certainly is the talk of the town." Unlike my husband, I was in no mood for silliness.

"According to Lieutenant Matthew Cusak," (it was my turn to read aloud), "Harrison Fowler most likely died of natural causes; however, the exact cause of death will not be confirmed until Dr. Loo releases the findings of the autopsy. Mr. Fowler was the latest in a series of managers employed by the Sleepy Hollow Country Club of Seville, Indiana. Mrs. Vernon Higgins, the board president and spokesperson for the club, said Mr. Fowler will be hard to replace, and she will miss him dearly."

Charlie snorted. "I'll bet she will. I don't think you're going to learn anything new from that article other than Matt's statement that the deceased's sister is resting comfortably at Garrison General Hospital."

"Sister? What sister? Are you telling me that Stella Robeson is Harrison Fowler's sister? Well, I'll be damned." In my surprise, I dropped the last triangle of toast directly into the waiting, open mouth of our four-legged, tail-wagging, garbage disposal.

"So that's why she was so upset when he died. Harrison and Stella, brother and sister. How about that. I never would have guessed it in a million years. I'll bet they decided to keep it a secret so that Harrison couldn't be accused of nepotism. It makes me wonder what else our son-in-law knows and isn't telling me."

"Oh for chrissakes, leave the guy alone. He's got enough on his plate without having to deal with a mother-in-law who thinks she's Seville's answer to Christie's Miss Marple."

From the smug look on Charlie's face, I could tell that unlike me, my husband was quite pleased with the analogy.

"I beg to differ with you, chum. I'm a lot younger than Jane Marple, and the only thing I've ever knitted is my brow. If you insist on comparing me to one of Christie's fictional detectives, might I suggest Hercule

Poirot. Like me, he is extremely intelligent, and if memory serves me right, he smokes the occasional cigarette."

"Well Mrs. Smartypants," said Charlie, getting up from the table and removing his golf jacket from the back of the chair, "I'd love to stay and discuss literary characters with you, but I'm already late picking up Denny. He gets so antsy when he thinks we might not get in a full eighteen holes. I don't know why. Hell, this time of year we've virtually got the course to ourselves."

Reaching down, he ran his hand over Pesty's tangled, fussy coat, sending a squall of fur skidding across the kitchen floor. "If you're looking for something to do today, she could do with a bit of grooming. Hey, if Denny calls, and I'm sure he will, tell him that I'm on the way."

He made me an offer before disappearing out the kitchen door. "After that great breakfast, I owe you something. If you play your cards right and stay out of trouble, which means no sleuthing, we'll go out to dinner tonight. My treat."

"Really?" I replied dryly. "And where might we be dining? Max's Diner?" I was almost positive that we wouldn't be going to the dumpy diner, but with Charlie you never know.

"You got it kid," he laughed, "it's hash night." And with that, he was gone. His car had barely reached the end of the driveway when the telephone began to ring. Anticipating Denny's phone call, I raced to answer it.

"Hello and don't panic," I instructed the caller, "he's on his way."

"Who's on his way? Where?" came the reply. "Is this the Hastings residence? Can you help me, or have I dialed the wrong number?" The female caller's voice was vaguely familiar. My inability to instantly match the voice with a face added to my self-inflicted predicament.

"Oh, I'm sorry," I said, "I thought you were someone else." It was a little late to bemoan the fact that I didn't have a separate business line. Surely, I had just offended a potential customer trying to get in touch with Designer Jeans. Other than a simple redo of an enclosed patio, scheduled for the end of the month, my business calendar was bare.

"You've reached the Hastings residence. This is Jean Hastings of Designer Jeans. Who's calling, please? How may I help you?"

The silence that followed was almost unbearable. Was the caller reevaluating her position, perhaps thinking the phone call was a mistake? Finally, she spoke, "Mrs. Hastings, this is Stella Robeson. You can help me by finding out who it was that murdered my dear brother."

"Oh boy," I said under my breath, "there goes dinner at the diner."

CHAPTER FOURTEEN

It was close to lunch time when Mary and I arrived at the hospital. "Visiting hours do not begin until one p.m.," we were curtly informed by the uniformed female volunteer seated behind the kidney-shaped, avocado-green, Formica-topped desk. The senior citizen's lavender-tinted elaborate coiffure was complemented, in an odd way, by the generous application of blue frosted eye shadow and glossy pink lipstick. Returning to her copy of *Soap Opera Newsy Notes,* the woman didn't make any effort to stop us when Mary and I headed for the bank of elevators that service the four floors of Garrison General Hospital.

Pressing the square indicator button, we positioned ourselves for a quick entrance as the middle of the three elevators opened its door and discharged a handful of hospital personnel. We stepped inside the vacated car. I was relieved to find that we would be its only passengers.

"Maybe we shouldn't interrupt Stella's lunch," said Mary as the elevator door slid closed and the car began to move. "I know when Denny was in here last year for his hernia operation, he threw a fit if anyone even phoned him while he was having lunch. How he can eat so much and never gain any weight is a mystery to me. Why, if I ever . . . oh my stars," Mary cried with alarm, "we're going down, not up. Gin, do something quick. There's no one to visit in the basement except dead people." Mary's roly-poly body quivered at the thought.

"Or Doctor Sue Lin Loo," I answered as the elevator came to an abrupt stop. "After all, Designer Jeans did redecorate the medical examiner's office when Pete Gladstone left and Loo took over. What's wrong with checking to see if she's pleased with the results?"

"That job was finished almost a year ago, for pity's sake." Mary shook her head in disbelief, causing a lock of her hair to escape from its tortoiseshell clasp. The delicate hair ornament had lost the battle to restrain Mary's mass of white curls. "I'm sure if she wasn't pleased, you would've heard something by now. Doctor Loo is going to think we're either senile or just plain crazy."

The elevator door opened slowly and revealed the first of several obstacles we would encounter in my pursuit of information relating to Stella's request.

"Well, well. Look who's here. If it isn't Grandmaw Jean and her trusty sidekick, Auntie Mary." The speaker was Matt. Both he and Sergeant Rosen stepped inside the elevator car, successfully blocking our exit. "And what may I ask, are you two charming ladies up to today? You wouldn't be playing detective again, now would you?"

Although his manner was light and breezy, my son-in-law didn't fool me. Behind that friendly facade, his policeman's mind was processing the scene. I had to think fast before Mary blurted out the truth, something she's prone to do when caught in a tight situation.

"We're here to donate blood," I said as casually as I could. I held my breath and hoped that Mary's open mouth wouldn't give me away.

"The place for that is still on the main floor," Matt countered, "right, Sergeant?"

A man of few words, the former Green Beret with the bushy mustache grunted and nodded his shaved egg-shaped head.

"Oh really?" said Mary, the picture of innocence. "You know, at our age, it's so easy to get confused."

I was surprised. I didn't think Mary would rise to the occasion. That she had more to say was another surprise.

"Why, I can't begin to tell you how many times Jean and I have gotten lost in the new mall over in Springvale. Only last week, we went there for the big annual white sale at Mayer Brothers and wouldn't you know, we took a wrong turn. We must have spent at least fifteen minutes looking for the linen department before we were saved by an understanding sales clerk. If it hadn't been for his help, we'd probably still be wandering around in men's underwear."

"Is that so?" said Matt. Somehow, he managed not to laugh. "Well, we wouldn't want anything like that to happen today, seeing that you're on such a humanitarian mission."

The elevator door slid closed, taking the four of us on the short journey to the hospital's main floor. "Sergeant Rosen will be more than happy to escort the two of you to the proper location. Won't you, Sid?"

"No problem, Lieutenant," said the stoic law officer. "I know how it is. My grandmother wears one of those doo-dads around her neck so she can get help twenty-four-seven. Maybe that's something you ladies should look into."

Thirty minutes later, Mary and I were downing apple juice and nibbling vanilla wafers while we recuperated in one of the hospital's curtained cubicles. Garrison General's blood supply had just been increased by two pints, thanks to us. Our unplanned introduction to the world of phlebotomy proved more interesting than traumatic.

Mary, who has a tendency to dramatize even the most mundane event, was uncharacteristically mellow. "You know something, Jean, that wasn't so bad after all. In fact, I'd say it was pretty easy. I don't know why more people don't give blood."

I suspected that Mary's newly acquired, calm demeanor stemmed either from my offer to buy lunch, or from the attending nurse's admonition that we were not to engage in any type of strenuous exercise or physical labor for the next twelve hours. Mary was quite pleased with the wad of sterile cotton nestled in the crook of her left arm. A three-inch-long strip of white adhesive held the small pad in place. This temporary medical dressing was proudly displayed by Mary as we followed signs, arrows, and our noses to the hospital's cafeteria.

With any hope of gleaning information from Doctor Loo dashed, I was anxious to move on and meet with Stella. After bolting down some pasta salad, a bran muffin, and a diet soda, I found myself waiting while Mary leisurely consumed a tuna salad–laden croissant, a cup of cheese-topped French onion soup, a large square of buttered corn bread, a fudge nut brownie, and a thick chocolate milkshake.

"Say Mar, how's the battle of the bulge coming along?" I asked as she noisily sucked the dregs of the ice cream concoction through a plastic straw.

"About the same as your battle with those cancer-causing coffin nails." Mary smiled sweetly, her blue eyes staring into mine. "Gotcha, Gin. Tofu sundae, my ass."

"Visiting hours at Garrison General have now begun. Those wishing to visit with a patient must first obtain a pass from the volunteer at the front desk located in the main lobby. Thank you." The disembodied voice seemed to be coming from the ceiling, wafting over the walls.

In accordance with the illustrated instructions posted on the walls of the cafeteria, we dutifully tidied up the table, taking care to deposit our trays of soiled dishes and flatware on the designated stainless-steel counter. Chores finished, we were about to leave when Doctors Loo and Parker, along with Matt and Sergeant Rosen, barged through the cafeteria's double doors. Doing all it could to keep up with the fast-moving foursome was a small entourage of medical and police personnel.

Bypassing the bountiful selection of food, the entire group headed straight for the huge silver urn of coffee and the stack of clean, ceramic mugs. Busy with the dispensing of coffee and reaching over one another for spoons, sugar packets, and powdered cream, no one in the group acknowledged our presence. This was fine with me. It made our exit quick and easy. Besides, I didn't have any desire for a second confrontation with my son-in-law, which might have led to god knows what, or as Mary feared, some unscheduled surgery.

Back at the front desk, Ms. Purple Poof Hair-do demanded, "Name?" Setting down the magazine, the keeper of the gate placed her hand on the knob of a small, plastic index wheel. Using her long, scarlet-lacquered fingernails, the woman impatiently tapped the side of the device while she waited for an answer.

"Mary England and Jean Hastings," said Mary, sounding more like a faltering adolescent than a forceful, mature adult. Mary doesn't do well with authority figures, even minor ones.

"You're only permitted to visit one patient at a time. So who's it going to be? The English one or Jane Hasty?" Poor Mary. The volunteer's impatience with her was growing, and Mary's hesitancy was only making it worse. Turning to me, the woman rolled her eyes and repeated her original demand: "Name?"

"Stella Robeson," I answered in a crisp monotone, determined to avoid locking horns with her. The volunteer was oblivious to the fact that she, not Mary, was the root cause of their misunderstanding. A quick spin of the wheel by the irksome woman resulted in the passes needed to enter Stella's third-floor hospital room. Grabbing Mary by the arm, I headed for the nearest elevator.

We didn't have any trouble locating the room, but we did have trouble locating Stella. Her bed was empty. When her roommate mistook us for a couple of church ladies, the confused woman began reciting passages from the Bible. It was time for us to retreat.

Returning to the hallway, we made a few wrong turns before arriving at the nurses' station, where we received some distressing news: Stella, who had been hopitalized for observation the night before, had suffered a stroke shortly after breakfast that morning and had been transferred to the intensive care unit.

"No visitors allowed. Doctor Parker's orders," we were told by the nurse on duty. She shifted her attention back to a stack of medical charts and a mound of thick file folders. Looking up from her work, the nurse was perplexed to find that we hadn't taken our leave.

The middle-aged woman appeared to be more tired than angry. "I haven't any other information for you about your friend. I've told you everything I can. Honest."

I was almost ashamed of myself, but I had two questions that needed to be answered. First, was Stella able to talk? And second, what did she say, if anything, right before or after the stroke? I practically got on my knees and begged the nurse for the answers.

"No to the first question, and I think the same for your second one," the nurse replied. "I'm not positive, though. You see, we're so understaffed, sometimes it's even hard to remember your own name." The overhead fluorescent lighting emphasized the dark circles under the fatigued woman's deep-set eyes.

"I know what you mean. My sister Nelly in Iowa says the same thing," I said, stepping firmly on Mary's foot. Luckily, her cry of pain was lost in the loud crash of breaking glass. The jarring noise came from an alcove located behind the station. The nurse ignored the intrusion.

"I'll bet you're as underpaid and unappreciated as my sister," I prattled on. "Nelly says being a nurse is the hardest job in the whole world." I threw in the last part for good measure, but also because I believe it.

"That's for damn sure," she said, leaning back in her chair. "I'd like to see how long these doctors would last, working the hours we do and for the same pay." Lowering her voice, she glanced around warily. "If we nurses goofed off as much as they do, this entire hospital would be in total chaos."

I did a great deal of head nodding as the woman poured out her grievances. When the litany concluded, she called out for someone named Tiffany. Immediately, a young student nurse stepped out of the alcove and into the desk area. Believing she was in trouble regarding the glass mishap, Tiffany began to apologize most profusely.

"All right, that's enough of that," scolded the senior nurse. "Try to be a little more careful next time you wash the doctors' coffeepot. There should be an extra carafe in the bottom drawer of one of the file cabinets. You can look for it later. Right now, these two nice ladies need your help. They want to know about their friend, three-o-two, bed one. Since you were with her at the time, maybe you can tell them if she said anything right before or after she took ill."

The student nurse seemed puzzled. "Said something? Like what?" Overplucked eyebrows, wide-set eyes, and a kewpie doll mouth gave Tiffany's oval-shaped face an expression of permanent surprise, even when she was deep in thought.

"You tell me," I said, realizing that this was not going to be easy. I would have had a better chance at success if I had asked her to recite the Gettysburg Address. "Please try to remember. It's really important to me."

"And to her sister Nelly the nurse," Mary added in payback for my trouncing on her toes. I ignored her suggestion that I show the two nurses a photo of the nonexistent Nelly.

We waited for a long time while Tiffany made an effort to retrieve something, anything, from her short-term memory file.

"Oh nuts," she said, shrugging her narrow shoulders. Apparently, the file was empty.

"Well, thanks for trying," I said, hiding my disappointment as best I could. "Come on, Mary, we mustn't take up any more of these busy people's time. It certainly was nice talking with you both."

"No, no," Tiffany objected as we turned to leave. "That's what you wanted to know. Your friend had just hung up the phone when I walked in to take temps. She was going on and on about trouble at some Halloween doings. It had something to do with her brother or mother. I don't know, 'cause I wasn't paying much attention to what she was saying. When it hit her, the stroke I mean, bed two started praying so loud, it was hard to hear anything." Tiffany hesitated before going on, "Actually, I told bed two to shut up. I hated being so mean but everything happened so fast. It was scary. One minute bed one was fine and then, bam! She turns red and gets all stiff like. Then, right before she flops back on the pillow, she says it, she says, 'Oh nuts.' Can I go now?"

The ride down in the elevator was uncomfortably crowded with departing visitors. By the time we reached the lobby, I felt closer to my fellow passengers than I'd ever wanted, in particular, the kid with the runny nose. While I did my best to ignore his constant snuffling, Mary engaged his mother in conversation. When we reached the main floor, I headed straight for the nearest exit leading to the parking lot.

Once outside, I smoked a cigarette and waited for Mary. Five minutes passed but still no Mary. I was about to unlock the van when she finally appeared. Irritated that I'd been kept waiting, I sarcastically inquired about the kid's cold.

"For your information, Jean, the boy has an allergy. His mom said they ran tests to find out why he was so congested and wheezy. The problem turns out to be the boy's pet chinchilla. When I told her I've never heard of anyone being allergic to that kind of dog, she laughed. Go figure."

I did. It was easy. Mary had confused the chinchilla, a South American rodent, with the chihuahua, the popular pooch from Mexico. I was debating whether or not I should bring this to her attention when Mary abruptly changed the subject.

"Would you mind stopping at the market on the way home? I promised Denny I'd pick up some Ovaltine for him. He goes nuts when we're out of it. He really loves the stuff."

"Holy Moses, that's it Mary! That's what killed Harrison!" In the excitement of the moment, I'd accidentally hit the panic button on the van's remote control keychain, setting off the blaring horn alarm. It wasn't the smartest thing to do in a hospital parking lot.

"What? He died from drinking Ovaltine?" Although she had to shout in order to be heard over the din, the amazement in Mary's voice came through loud and clear. "Oh my stars. And here I've been giving it to Denny all these years."

"Oh dear God, there's nothing wrong with drinking Ovaltine," I shouted back, fumbling to turn off the alarm. "The man was allergic to nuts. Just being near them was enough to do him in. Nuts, Mary. That's what Stella was trying to say. Think about all the changes made in the club's menu. The new menu had no nuts, nowhere, no how. It was healthy, all right, but for who? Harrison, that's who. If somebody figured out Harrison had a food allergy and deliberately fixed it so that he would unknowingly come in contact with nuts, then Stella could be right. Somebody could have killed her brother."

"Hey, what's going on out here? Turn that blasted alarm off and stop your caterwaulin'. In case you two didn't notice, this is an official quiet zone and it's against the law to disturb the peace." The man yelling at us was a stern, humorless security guard. "You look like a couple of real troublemakers to me. Let's see some identification," he demanded, "and I ain't going to tell you again. Turn off that damn alarm."

I was struggling to turn off the alarm, pull out my driver's license, and shout down the guard when Matt and Sergeant Rosen crossed the parking lot. They were headed for their unmarked police car. Mary waved madly, expecting them to come to our rescue. Instead, the two police officers ignored her and our predicament. "Oh fudge," she called out as the smiling duo drove out of sight. "Or should I say, oh nuts."

CHAPTER FIFTEEN

I arrived home to an unkempt Kees who was in a foul mood due to my failure to produce a napkin-wrapped, edible surprise from the depths of my leather shoulder purse. In a futile attempt to placate her, I offered Pesty a Dandy Diet dog biscuit, which she politely refused.

"Sorry, girl," I said, tossing the rocklike object in her bowl, "but I had to stop and see an old friend of ours, Horatio Bordeaux. You remember him, don't you? You know, Fifi's owner."

The mere mention of the cat's name was enough to cause the Keeshond's fur to bristle. Obviously, Pesty hadn't forgotten the faux gentle, Persian feline with the long, sharp claws. The two pampered pets met last year when Designer Jeans redesigned Horatio's home office, transforming it into a workplace that was handicap accessible, comfortable, and efficient.

A widower, Horatio Bordeaux once had a promising career with the Central Intelligence Agency. That was before diabetes robbed him of some of his sight and most of his toes. Twelve years ago he returned to Seville and began teaching classes in political science at Sev-Vale College until his retirement two years earlier.

Never one to sit back in his wheelchair and watch the world go by, Horatio started his own business on the web, specializing in locating hard-to-find-people, places, and things. If I was going to solve a murder mystery, I would need all the help I could get, which is why I stopped to see him after dropping off Mary, and the Ovaltine, at her house. To someone as well-connected as Horatio, getting the info I wanted would be a piece of cake. At least that's what he told me. He also promised to get back to me shortly. I hoped he was right on both counts.

"Maybe you'll have better luck with Charlie when he comes home," I said to Pesty as she followed me up the stairs and into the bedroom, where we both settled down on the inviting, king-sized bed for a well-deserved nap. I didn't know what had tired me out more: donating blood, dealing with the nursing staff, the parking lot fiasco, or my meeting with Horatio. I promptly fell asleep.

Charlie arrived home a half hour later, waking me with a kiss and reviving the sleeping Pesty with a couple of soggy french-fried potatoes. I had to fight the urge to go back to sleep as I listened to Charlie's hole-by-hole replay of his three-dollar win over Denny. Offically, Sleepy Hollow had closed the course for the season. Only die-hards like Denny and Charlie continued to play it.

Charlie was still talking as he stepped into the shower. "Hey Jean," he hollered over the noise of the gushing water, "you need to get out more. Do something different. Expand your horizons. Meet new people. You always get bored when you're not working on some design project. That's why you took a nap today. You weren't tired, you were bored." Yeah, right.

That evening, JR and Matt decided to join us at Giant Joe's Steak House, where the salads, baked potatoes, biscuits, and desserts are almost as big as the steaks. The popular western-style restaurant is located in Bard's Valley, Matt's old stomping grounds. Much to our delight, we were seated immediately despite a lengthy waiting list.

The attractive hostess remembered Matt from his salad days, having attended many of the same beer bashes and pizza parties. We weren't in the smoking section, yet I didn't complain. We could've had a table in the cigar bar, where smoking is permitted, but I checked it out and discovered smoke so thick that even I didn't want to sit in there.

We took our time with the steaks, skipped dessert, but lingered over gigantic mugs of hot tea laced with honey.

"Boy, that was the best steak I've had in a long time," Charlie declared. "My better half wanted to go to Max's for the hash. I had a hell of time talking her out of it," he said with a straight face.

"You've got to be kidding," JR gasped, not realizing her father was doing just that — kidding. "Honestly, Mom, you really surprise me sometimes. Like today: you and Aunt Mary going over to the hospital and donating blood. When Matt told me that and how you almost went to the morgue by mistake, I could hardly believe it."

"Yeah, your mother is just full of surprises," said her father, giving me a dark look along with the dinner bill. He also gave me the distinct impression that once we were alone, the subject would be discussed in greater detail.

The final total, which I paid in full and in cash, included an automatic hefty gratuity for parties of four or more and gave new meaning to Giant Joe's emphasis on largess.

The following morning, Charlie and Denny again joined the smattering of golfers out on the course. They were determined to play as many rounds as possible before Mother Nature turned the tree-lined fairways into a temporary haven for winter sports enthusiasts.

While a carefree Charlie tromped around the golf course, I was engaged in a battle of wits with Pesty. She refused to come out from under the kitchen table once she spied the hated grooming brush in my hand. She was saved by the bell when the telephone rang.

The caller was Matt. Not chatty by nature, he got right to the point. "After our little run-in at Garrison General yesterday, followed by your getting stuck with the bill last night, I feel I owe you one. I thought you might like to know that Loo says Fowler died from anaphlaxis," said Matt, his tongue tripping ever so slightly over the medical term.

"So he did have a severe allergy. What did he take for it? Epinephrine? Where the hell was his emergency kit? He had to have one. Did you search his office?" I hoped that I sounded nonchalant. "Any idea what triggered the fatal reaction or is Loo still checking it out?"

"Hey, Jean, let it go. As it stands now, it looks like death from natural causes. Okay?" He tried to hide it, but I could tell that he was getting annoyed with me.

"Then that about wraps it up, doesn't it?" I said, removing a strand of dog hair from the corner of my mouth. I started to say something more, but was interrupted by Matt.

"It does as far as you're concerned. Listen, all I can say is that the death is still under investigation. I thought we had a deal. I don't stick my nose in your business and you keep yours out of mine."

Not wanting to end our conversation on a sour note, Matt insisted that the next time the four of us dined out, it would be his treat. "But let's not go to Max's Diner. I hear the food there is a real killer," he joked. "Bye-bye, Grandmaw."

"Matt, wait. Don't hang up," I cried, but it was too late. Without the aid of my reading glasses, I proceeded to select two wrong options before finding the correct one on the cordless kitchen phone. The repetitive beeping of a busy signal blocked my attempt to reconnect with Matt. For a fee, a recorded voice offered to continue trying the number and call me back when the line was free. I hung up before the message was finished, resenting an intrusion being passed off as a service, and a relatively expensive one at that.

On second thought, I decided, it was probably best that Matt's call ended when it did. If I was right about Harrison's deadly allergy to nuts, it didn't prove that he was murdered. Also, I would have had to explain how and where I'd gotten my information, and why I had pursued the matter in the first place. The last thing I wanted to do was to alienate my son-in-law.

Replacing the phone in its base and returning the grooming brush to the shelf in the utility room, I wondered what to do next. I thought about the twist Harmon had put on the old adage about letting sleeping dogs lie. He had said something about letting the old dog rest in peace. Was it a reminder of sorts to himself? Or was it a precognitive warning meant for me?

Chapter Sixteen

Starting my second cup of coffee that morning, I found myself wishing Stella had given me more to go on than just her belief that Harrison was murdered. If only she had been more forthright during our phone conversation instead of insisting on a face-to-face meeting. Nuts just about summed up the entire matter.

Finishing my coffee, I looked around for my cigarette case. Normally, the case would have been within easy reach, but I had been to so many smoke-free places of late and with so many smoke-free people, I had temporarily mislaid it. Thinking it was probably in my leather shoulder bag, I began searching the house for the purse. Pesty joined in, cautiously stopping a few paces behind me each time I entered and exited a room.

"Don't look at me like that," I said to her while I explored the dark recesses of the front hall closet (a favorite depository for clutter). "I'm not having a senior moment. I'm merely acting like a woman."

The little furball plopped down on the hallway's cool slate floor. It was a move designed to conserve her energy.

"Men hunt for car keys and women search for purses. Too bad I can't find the damn thing. Besides my cigarettes, there's a doggy bag with a Texas-size biscuit in it."

Letting out a yelp so shrill I thought I might have accidentally stepped on one of her paws, Pesty dashed out of sight only to return dragging the heavy leather carry-all by its strap. Had I mentioned the doggy bag sooner, it would have saved a lot of time and trouble.

While Pesty slept, probably dreaming of buttery biscuits, I sat down at the kitchen table, lit a cigarette, and studied the list Mary had written on the back of the Halloween card.

NAME	GENRE
Dr. Parker	*fishing*
Chief Stevens	*true crime*
Tom MacNulty	*paranormal*
Jason Bowman	*chemistry*
Vanessa Higgins	*beauty*
Vern Higgins	*gardening*

Cord Stanford	*finance*
Harrison Fowler	*health*
Stella Robeson	*cooking*
Billy Birdwell	*science*

At the time the list had been compiled, the concern was with Harmon's death, not Harrison's. Now I wondered if the two deaths were somehow connected. Maybe, maybe not. Did the list hold the answer, or even a clue? Another maybe, maybe not.

If either man had been poisoned then books purchased by Jason Bowman or Billy Birdwell or even Vernon Higgins could have been a factor. And what about Chief Stevens's choice of reading material? Was his interest in true crime above the norm? He certainly had a history of rather bizarre behavior. But was it murderous? I didn't think so. If drawing smiley faces on the duty roster, issuing a be on the lookout (BOLO) for a missing cat, and posting cookie recipes on the bulletin board were signs of a killer, then Rollie Stevens qualified hands down. When Cardinal John Henry Newman, the scholary English cleric, gave the advice to act on what we have, not on what we wish, he must've had a lot more to work with than I did.

The list was getting me nowhere. I was

about to toss the card in the trash compactor when something caught my attention. The paranormal? Why would a levelheaded guy like Tom MacNulty be interested in things that go bump in the night? Perhaps I should talk to him. It wasn't much, but it was a starting point of sorts. Maybe Newman was right after all.

A quick phone call to Mary confirmed that the burly bartender was a familiar sight on the Seville park walking trail. According to Mary, Mac was a devoted dog owner who used the trail twice a day as a place to exercise Mave, his beloved Irish wolfhound. The dog was a gift from Luanne long before Gary Winslow came on the scene. Mean-spirited gossips claimed that Mac paid more attention to the dog than he did to Luanne, and that Mave was the real cause of the couple's breakup.

The late-morning sun had ducked behind a growing mass of clouds, marring an otherwise clear sky. The moment the sun disappeared, the northern breeze increased in velocity, causing gangs of multihued, fallen leaves to run for cover in nearby nooks and crannies. There isn't a better place than the park in all of Seville for witnessing the change of seasons. But I wasn't there for that purpose. I was there hoping to cross paths with Tom MacNulty.

Needing a reason to be in the vicinity, I brought a leashed Pesty with me. My thinking was that she might actually enjoy being out in the fresh air, which she did — for about the first five minutes. The remainder of the time she spent huddled against me as we sat side by side on the hard, wrought-iron park bench.

We watched in silence as bicyclists peddled past an array of walkers, joggers, and sprinters using the narrow, tree-lined trail. Since school was in session, there was almost a total absence of children and teenagers. It was also a workday, so the trail was populated, for the most part, by older adults not generally considered to be prime players in today's youth-oriented society. I was in awe of the physical fitness and stamina these energetic senior citizens demonstrated. Clearly, the little Kees and I were out of shape and out of place. Like a couple of unrepentant sinners in the Promised Land, we didn't belong. I knew it and so did Pesty.

With no sign of our prey, or returning sunshine, I suggested that we call it quits and head for home. Pesty agreed, licking my face in gratitude. We were within a few feet of my van, which I'd parked in the lot nearest the trail's entrance, when someone shouted for me to stop. Turning around, I was nearly bowled over by the biggest dog I'd ever seen.

"I'll bet you're Mave," I said to the massive animal. Pesty immediately dropped flat to the ground and tried to pass herself off as an inanimate object. In her rush to protect life and limb (hers, not mine), Pesty failed to notice that the dog was accompanied by her master.

"Gee, Mrs. Hastings, I'm real sorry. When Mave saw you and your dog, she took off. It's my fault more than hers. I should have had her on a much shorter leash. I hope she didn't scare your little pooch too badly," said Mac, looking down at the motionless blob whose ancestors were valued by Dutch barge owners for their ability to ward off strangers. The bartender's apology was followed by his offer to treat me to a cafe mocha at the recently opened Koffee Kabin located across the town square.

Accepting the apology and the offer, I agreed to meet Mac at the coffeehouse in ten minutes, giving him enough time to take Mave home.

I waited until Mac and his dog disappeared around the corner before prying Pesty from the pavement. I carried her in my arms to the van. Some much-needed words of assurance from me that she had indeed acted wisely, followed by a drink of bottled water, helped to calm her down. The Kees then collapsed in a furry heap, exhausted by the harrowing incident. For Pesty, it was a senior moment, proving such occurrences are not limited to human beings.

At the Koffee Kabin, while Mac placed our order at the counter, I managed to appropriate a clean, empty table in spite of the lunch hour crowd. Shortly thereafter, Mac returned with two stout, imitation pewter mugs of steaming cafe mocha. The style of the mugs was in keeping with the Koffee Kabin's colonial decor.

Between sips of the sweet, frothy coffee and snippets of light talk, I tried to figure out how I was going to steer the conversation toward the paranormal. I was struggling with the problem when Mac came up with the solution.

"Mrs. Hastings," he began, ignoring three busybodies who were seated nearby and straining to catch what he was saying, "do you believe in ghosts?"

Holy Cardinal Newman, I said to myself, this is almost too easy.

Thirty minutes and two more coffees

later, I had the whole story. Mac claimed that there were strange, unexplained happenings in the club's west wing. They began on the Monday before Harmon's death. Most of the weird activity took place in the storage room and in the bar area. Items had been mysteriously moved or were missing. Lacking a logical explanation as to who or what had caused these disturbances, Mac reluctantly concluded that Sleepy Hollow was haunted.

"All this spooky stuff started the day Fowler had some kind of meeting in his office. Nobody else was supposed to be in the club so I started checking around. You and JR were busy in the dining room and the meeting was still going on. I know, 'cause I walked down the east corridor and I could hear them arguing. When the meeting broke up, I was in the foyer. Jason Bowman all but busted his butt getting out of there. Mr. Brinker came out of the office a few minutes later and stopped to visit with you and JR. I thought he looked upset."

Swallowing a mouthful of coffee, Mac made a face and pushed the mug aside. "Shit, I hate cold coffee."

"What did you say?" I asked incredulously, almost upsetting the entire contents of the table.

"What? Oh, sorry, but I really do hate cold coffee," Mac replied, apologizing for his spontaneous use of the expletive.

"No, no. What you said about Jason. He was there?" I found this bit of information more interesting than Mac's ghost.

It was Mac's turn to ask the questions. "Yes, he was there, but like I said, he left way before Mr. Brinker did. Why? Do you think he's got something to do with the ghost? Like maybe he brought it into the place? Now that I think about it, the guy is kind of odd. He's always talking about the economy, politics, or taxes. You know, depressing kinds of stuff."

"Did you happen to hear what the argument was about? Accidentally, of course," I added, giving Mac an out if he was reluctant to admit that he'd engaged in eavesdropping.

"Yes and no. Something to do with morality, or maybe it was mortality. Anyway, lots of really snotty remarks were made about Fowler's track record at some old people's home. To tell the truth, I was hoping they were going to fire him. I really didn't like the guy even before he started dating Luanne. But since Mrs. Higgins and Mr. Stanford weren't at the meeting, I guess his job wasn't on the line."

Mac ran his hand over his craggy face. His blue-green eyes looked troubled and tired. "Honest to God, I was so freaked out about what was going on in the west wing, I didn't care if they were killing each other. Did I tell you about the pictures in the bar? Half of them were hanging upside-down. Now that's spooky. Some say it's the sign of the devil." Luanne Winslow's unexpected appearance in the Koffee Kabin brought all further inquiries to a halt. No longer having Mac's undivided attention, I gave way to lovers in love and waved Luanne over to the table.

"Here, Luanne," I insisted, gathering up my purse and keys, "take my seat. I was just leaving."

Passing the counter, I snatched a pumpkin square and dropped a dollar bill in its place. "Keep the change," I called out to the startled clerk as the door swung shut. It was then that I noticed the sign in the window: PUMPKIN SQUARES — 3 FOR $5.00. Oblivious to the fact that my math left a lot to be desired, a pleased Pesty gobbled up the scrumptious treat before resuming her nap.

CHAPTER SEVENTEEN

"Yes, I was with Harmon when he met with Mr. Fowler. It was Harmon's idea that I be there," Jason Bowman said. "He said he needed a witness. I was on my lunch hour and couldn't stay for the entire meeting. As to what was discussed, I don't think it's my place to say other than it was a private matter between Harmon and Mr. Fowler. There wasn't any argument, at least not in my presence. I'm sorry, I really must hang up now; Valley Labs frowns on employees receiving personal calls during business hours." The phone clicked and he was gone.

I made two more quick calls before returning the cell phone to its case. Once that was done, I drove down the alley and made my way back to the downtown area. If I hurried, I could pick up Mary, drive to Springvale, and be home in time to throw something together for supper.

Parking the van in the space marked EN-

GLAND DELIVERIES ONLY, I ran up the ramp and pressed the door release button. Too impatient to wait for the ancient, overhead door to complete its excruciatingly slow, creaking journey from sidewalk to ceiling, I ducked under it. From my crouched position I could hear Mary's voice.

"And back here, we have an even bigger selection of mattress sets. If you care to look around, my sister-in-law, the nimble Mrs. Hastings, will be glad to help you. Won't you, Jean dear?"

Even though Mary managed to suppress her surprise, the would-be customers, a dour-looking elderly couple, did not. Fearful of being left in the clutches of a half-human, half-crab salesperson, they headed straight for the furniture store's main showroom and its Main Street exit.

It was an effort, but I managed to extradite myself from the back-breaking position. "Boy, for a couple of old folks, they moved damn quick. Say, Mar, speaking of quick, Denny really should do something about that relic of a delivery door. It's sooo slow."

Twenty minutes later, a piqued Mary was in the passenger seat of the van as we headed east on the interstate toward Springvale, Indiana, and Safe Harbor, a private nursing home specializing in the care of elderly women.

"I know it matters little to you, but we are in the middle of our biggest sales promotion. You should thank your lucky stars that Herbie Waddlemeyer was nice enough to cover for me on his day off, otherwise I wouldn't be able to go with you on what is probably a wild goose chase."

Aware that Mary hadn't finished chewing me out, I kept my mouth shut and my eyes on the road.

"And what kind of entrance was that, Gin? Who do you think you are? The Queen of Egypt?"

A history major in my early college years, I couldn't resist. "Cleopatra made her entrance rolled up in a rug, or so the story goes."

"Oh yeah? Well, I'll bet she came through the front door and not the delivery dock. Honestly, you really looked like a kook. Mr. and Mrs. Swensen are probably still running and are halfway to Indianapolis by now."

An unexpected ripple of laughter washed over Mary, catching me in its wake. I waited for it to recede before bringing her up to speed on what I'd learned from Matt's phone call, my meeting with Mac, and the short phone conversation I'd had with Jason Bowman. I told her that while not denying that there had been an argument that day, since it was between Harrison and Harmon, "Jason feels that it's none of his or my business."

"Okay but why this trip to some Springvale nursing home?" Mary wanted to know as she switched the radio dial from station to station.

"Well, for starters, that's where Harrison was employed prior to signing on with the country club. It also happens to be the place where Harmon's mother, like Jason's mother, spent her last days. Even though he abhorred violence of any sort, the Harmon I knew would never take the mistreatment of anyone, especially his own mother, lightly. Remember how upset he was when those fraternity pledges were paddled 'til their buns were bloody blobs? He personally led the campaign to ban the fraternity from the campus of Sev-Vale College."

After taking a moment to digest what I'd said, Mary wanted to know what Matt had to say when I told him about Stella and the nuts. Unable to find a golden oldie, rock 'n roll station, she pushed the radio's Off button, something I greatly appreciated. I couldn't have handled Mary's questions, lane closures, and Motown's greatest hits all at the same time.

"If you mean did I tell him about Stella calling me and my theory about ground peanuts in the special mix used to rim the Bloody Mary glasses? No, I didn't. He hung up before I had the chance to tell him anything. Besides, I worked out the how of the murder, and I am inclined to believe that it was a murder, when I was sitting in the park with Pesty."

Nearing the turn-off for Springvale, I cautioned Mary to keep an eye out for Lake Avenue or Water Street. Directions to Safe Harbor included the usual "you can't miss it" but of course, we did. On our third go-'round, we finally arrived at our destination.

"My stars, this is some place," Mary remarked as I swung the van into a parking spot between a sleek, black Jaguar convertible and a spiffy, silver BMW. "The cost of spending your last years here must be murder. It looks like one of those quaint New England fishing villages where all the tourists are either rich or famous. I can't wait to see the inside."

Everything about Safe Harbor, from the miniature lighthouses flanking the entrance, to the widow's walk surrounding the top story of the stately, white clapboard structure, reflected the private institution's nautical theme.

We were escorted to a waiting room by a young, female employee who was fashionably dressed in a navy blue and white outfit. After inviting us to make ourselves comfortable, we were informed that the director, Ms. Rodgers, was aware of our arrival and would be available in a few minutes.

The determination of someone to bring the sea indoors was very much in evidence. The windowless room was flooded with artificial light streaming down from a chandelier that had once served as the wheel of a ship. Oil paintings depicting scenes of crashing waves, leaping dolphins, and seagulls lined three of the walls. A pair of crossed oars hung precariously on the remaining wall. The floor was covered in ankle-deep, plush sea-green carpeting. In the middle of the room, functioning as a table of sorts, sat a battered steamer trunk. The piece was plastered with travel decals. Seating was provided by wood and sailcloth deck chairs, each of which bore the stenciled message: PROPERTY OF THE H.M.S. *Pinafore.*

With my back and knees aching from my furniture store escapade, I chose to stand. Doubtful that the chairs could hold her weight, Mary chose to stand, too.

"My stars, Gin. Who decorated this place? Sinbad, the Sailor?" she quipped.

The invitation to proceed to the director's office immediately followed Mary's wisecrack. Knowing that Mary's mind was stuck somewhere on the high seas where pirate ships ruled the waves, I feared she'd lose all control once she learned that Ms. Rodger's given name was Jolee.

"Oh, like in Jolly Rodger," giggled Mary. "I hope she doesn't have a peg leg or an eye patch. Things like that can be a bit distracting, wouldn't you agree?"

I gave Mary a tissue to wipe the tears of laughter from her eyes and a stern warning that she either cool it or join Pesty in the van. Not wanting to miss anything, she promised to behave. That the director's office contained only a smattering of things nautical helped immensely.

CHAPTER EIGHTEEN

Ms. Rodgers sported neither a peg leg nor an eye patch. In fact, there wasn't really anything about the director that was worth noting other than she was neat, clean, and looked to be in her mid fifties. Her height, weight, and facial features were all average. The absence of color in her pale eyes and hair reminded me of a painted statue that had faded after years of watching over someone's garden.

On the ring finger of her long right hand was a plain band of gold. The narrow ring was the only piece of jewelry that she wore. Equally plain were the navy-blue jumper and the long-sleeved, white silk blouse that made up her outfit. The fabric and cut were such that it was obvious the outfit was an expensive one. Everything about Jolee Rodgers, from her choice in clothing to her choice in footwear (sensible walking shoes), spelled business in capital letters.

Once Mary and I were seated in mate chairs of maple, the director took her place in a captain's chair of the same wood. Ensconced behind a rather modest-sized, glass-topped desk, Jolee Rodgers listened attentively to what I had to say. When she responded to my inquiries, she did so without any prolonged hesitation. Subsequently, I learned that Sleepy Hollow's current board president, Vanessa Higgins, first met Harrison Fowler at a Safe Harbor open house.

"He so impressed your Mrs. Higgins with his managerial abilities that she was determined to hire him away. Naturally, Safe Harbor did what it could to keep Mr. Fowler and his sister, our cook, from leaving." The director's thin lips pressed together in a wry smile. "We even went so far as to match Mrs. Higgins's lucrative offer, but to no avail. As you already know, being such a close friend of the Fowler family, not only is Stella a marvelous cook, she is also a qualified dietitian. Everyone liked Stella."

Rubbing her forehead, Jolee Rodgers fell silent. I sensed that she'd reached a crossroads of sorts and was weighing her options before continuing. "I hate to say this, but I'll be honest with you. Harrison Fowler wasn't particularly liked by some of the staff. I believe his being a hard taskmaster, a perfectionist you might say, had a great deal to do with it."

The director clasped her hands to her flat chest as if in prayer and sighed deeply. "But oh my, the man was much loved by a good many of our residents. He would often sit with them for hours — and on his own time, mind you. He never seemed to tire of their stories. I guess you could say that he was a different man to different people."

That I could agree with, and I did before asking her about two residents, Mrs. Brinker and Mrs. Bowman. I wanted to know if they were among Harrison Fowler's favorites. Judging from the look on the director's face, I'd hit a sore spot.

"Unfortunately, as you know, both of the dear ladies are no longer with us. They passed on some months ago, maybe even a year. With so many of them leaving, and others taking their place, it is sometimes difficult to remember exact dates. I could look it up, I suppose."

"Oh, that won't be necessary," I said, trying to get the conversation back on track. "Harrison often spoke of the special bond he'd formed with many of the residents. Stella has asked me to give the eulogy for her brother, and I thought it would be a nice touch to mention some of Harrison's favorites by name," I lied, hoping God was too busy to notice.

Maybe God was busy but Mary wasn't. To her credit, she had the presence of mind to turn her audible astonishment into a phony hiccup. "My stars, I didn't expect that, the hiccup, I mean. Do continue with your inquiry, Jean dear."

"I will, Mary dear," I said, giving her my best, forced smile before turning my attention back to the director. "I thought maybe you could give me some idea of who and how many I should include."

Blotches of pink appeared on the director's cheeks, signaling her indignation. "Mrs. Hastings, I can only state in the strongest of terms that favoritism, like its opposite neglect, is not a part of Safe Harbor's curriculum. Although Harrison did spend more time with certain residents, favoritism had absolutely nothing to do with it.

"Safe Harbor strives hard to see that all residents are treated the same. If someone is claiming differently, it may stem from an inability to separate fact from fiction or past from present. It's a common problem among the elderly and something that our oldest resident, Rosalie Blumquist, is struggling with. The poor soul's convinced that Safe Harbor is a mobster-run gambling joint. When reality fades, it's often replaced by silly notions. I'm sorry, but I'm afraid I can't help you."

Pushing her chair away from the desk, the director stood up and extended her right hand first to me and then to Mary. The round of handshaking was accompanied by the usual exchange of social pleasantries. We were being dismissed, something I wasn't about to let happen.

"We'll be leaving now, but before we go, do you think we might visit with the oldest resident? With your permission, of course." I almost added, "Sister Mary Jolee," having the strong impression that this venerable form of address was once part of her life.

Checking the time on the schoolroom-type clock affixed above the office doorway, the director informed us that the resident in question would most likely be found in the general gathering room. "Residents," she explained, "often wait there for the dinner bell to chime. I'll give you ten minutes with her. Not a second longer. Remember, she is very elderly and tires easily."

Moving noiselessly across the office, the director opened the door and motioned to us to follow along. I could almost hear the soft, rhythmic click of swaying rosary beads as she led the way through a series of hallways before arriving at what looked like a cruise ship's salon, minus the cigarette smoke, dim lighting, and lounge lizards.

When people are segregated by age and gender, the end result is often a sameness that makes positive identification difficult, if not impossible, and has led to the unreliability of eyewitness testimony. It can also produce sketches of wanted criminals that bear an uncanny resemblance to your former brother-in-law or your kid's fifth grade math teacher. Perhaps Gertrude Stein's "Rose is a rose is a rose" is recognition of this insidious sameness rather than an exemplification of a particular writing style. Probably not.

Jolee Rodgers received an emergency page, which required her to hurry back to her office, leaving me and Mary to confront the problem of sameness on our own. We had to find a specific rose in a room full of roses. Not wanting to waste precious time, I decided the best way to solve the problem would be to call out Rosalie's name, which I did. Nothing. Unwilling to give up, I tried again and met with success.

Across the room a withered hand shot up, and a tiny voice called out, "I'm over here, toots." My hunch was right. I'd found the elusive Roxy Bloom.

CHAPTER NINETEEN

"Frankie. That's what I always called him. He hated being called Finky. Big Al hung that moniker on him after the coppers busted all the speaks in Chicago's Loop 'cept for Frankie's."

The birdlike old woman paused to sort through her thoughts and catch her breath.

Less than five feet tall and well under ninety pounds, Roxy Bloom, a.k.a. Rosalie Blumquist, had eluded notoriety and possible prosecution for murder by hiding in plain sight. Her hair, once a dazzling platinum (courtesy of frequent doses of peroxide), and cut in a daring shingle (a style popular in the flapper era), had long ago returned to its original drab brown. Nobody in Springvale ever paid any attention to the mousy, reference librarian with the sad, brown eyes and mannish hairdo.

"Nah, I didn't shoot him. I probably should have," said Roxy. Her cloudy eyes filled with tears. Taking the sleeve of her floral print duster, she dabbed at her sunken cheeks, ignoring the tiny rivulets of moisture that were poised on the edges of her nostrils.

"Sure, he used me. He used all us girls. What made it different between him and me was I knew it, but I didn't care. I had it real bad for the lug." Her wrinkled face glowed with the intensity of her emotions. For a fleeting moment, I caught a glimpse of Roxy, the flapper — wild, passionate, sexy, the epitome of flaming youth.

"Nah, I didn't shoot him," she repeated. "Even if I was in the same spot she was in, knocked up and all, I would've killed myself and spared him. That's how much I loved Frankie. Mrs. Rich Bitch never loved him. She blamed him for everything, even her bad luck at the tables. When Frankie told her he was gonna spill the beans to the dopey dud she married, that's when she pumped him full of lead."

If Roxy had been walking the line between two worlds, the past and the present, she seemed to be doing fine. But then she slipped.

"Goddamn it. You're from the D.A.'s office, ain't you?" Roxy was visibly agitated. "Or maybe you're workin' for her old man. Yeah, that's it. Well, you can tell Mr. Boston

Blueblood that I ain't talkin' to nobody." Clamping her hands over her mouth, Roxy shrank into the confines of her wheelchair and stared at the ceiling.

A short period of silence followed before Safe Harbor's oldest resident sprang back to life. Her milky eyes locked in on Mary, shutting me out.

"Heh, heh, ol' Roxy knows who you are," she cackled gleefully, pointing an arthritic finger at Mary. Shaking with excitement, the old woman's slipper-clad feet began drumming a tattoo on the tiled floor. "You're that big dame who yells to the customers. You get a kick out of callin' 'em suckers. Oh, that's you, all right. Tried to fool ol' Roxy, but I'm too smart for the likes of you."

Mary remained calm. Five years of witnessing the ravages of Alzheimer's disease (Denny's father was a victim), had taught her not to argue with the absurd.

"If J. Edgar's boys bother you too much, I'll tell my Frankie. He can put the fix in for you," croaked Roxy, moving further into another time and place. "Him and Big Al are just like brothers. Yeah, them two are just like brothers." Roxy's trembling head bobbed up and down, going slower and slower until her chin came to rest on her sagging bosom. She had fallen asleep. It was time for us to leave.

"Goodbye, Roxy Bloom. It was awfully nice meeting you," Mary whispered softly, knowing full well that she would not receive a response.

Removing the blue quilted coverlet from the back of the wheelchair, I gently placed it over the sleeping woman's lap, tucking it loosely around her fragile body. "And say goodbye to Rosalie Blumquist," I said, "wherever she is. It certainly was great visiting with you both. I wouldn't have missed it for the world."

The ride home to Seville was a long one with bumper-to-bumper traffic jams caused by a string of unexpected lane closures.

"I found our little visit to Safe Harbor to be very informative," I said to a sleepy Mary while we waited for the flag man to wave the van through yet another construction zone. "In spite of the director's denial, I think Harrison did have his favorites and that's probably what led to the argument that Mac overheard."

"I agree," said Mary, between yawns. "What do you make of what Roxy had to say? It's pretty obvious that she has a problem with reality, like Denny's dad had. Remember when he insisted that he won the Indy 500 in the Oscar Mayer Weiner-mobile?"

I was about to answer Mary when the flag man gave the signal for the van, and the long line of traffic behind it, to proceed with caution. With the return of the passing lane, a string of cars zoomed past us as if the van had been the cause of the delay. "Dotty or not, I think there's a ring of truth in what the old gal had to say, and I intend to check it out."

My words fell on deaf ears. Mary was fast asleep. The remainder of the drive home was long, silent, and uneventful.

CHAPTER TWENTY

"He wouldn't exactly be angry, more like really, really irritated." My daughter was speculating on her husband's reaction to my amateurish efforts to solve the mystery of Finky Dee's murder, Harmon Brinker's unfortunate accident, and Harrison Fowler's death. "But," said JR, putting her finger to her lips, "to be on the safe side, let's keep our voices down. I wouldn't want the twins telling their father that Grandma was sticking her nose in police business again."

We were in the kitchen of Kettle Cottage, clearing away the remains of a last-minute family pizza party. Charlie, Kerry, and Kelly had retreated to the den, where they quickly became involved in Charlie's latest computer game.

Coming home to an empty house and cold stove is not Charlie's idea of love and marriage. Earlier, in an attempt to track me down, he'd made a series of phone calls,

eventually reaching the always accommodating Herbie Waddlemayer at England's
Fine Furniture. From Herbie, Charlie
learned of our trip to Springvale, but not its
purpose. Assuming I'd gone shopping with
Mary and wouldn't make it home in time
to fix dinner, my husband took matters into
his own hands: He ordered a large cheese
pizza from Milano's. Next, he invited JR
and the twins to dinner at our house. Matt
had been invited as well but was unavail-
able. Charlie's timing was perfect. I arrived
home in time to pay the pizza delivery man.

I did feel a bit silly whispering in my own
home, but I agreed wholeheartedly with JR.
It would be better for all concerned to keep
my investigation private.

After bringing JR up to date, beginning
with Stella's phone call and ending with my
visit with Roxy Bloom, I waited while she
digested the flood of information.

"What put you on to Safe Harbor?" JR
wanted to know. "Was it because of what
Mac overheard? And why didn't Mr. Bowman want to tell you what Harrison and
Mr. Brinker discussed at the meeting?"

"Whoa, slow down, JR. I can only answer
one question at a time. To begin with, like
everyone else, I'd forgotten that Harmon
and Jason were distantly related. They were

third or fourth cousins, or something like that. Anyway," I said, helping myself to a cup of reheated coffee, "the two families weren't very close in life, yet in death they're interred in the same area. I happened to notice this when I attended Harmon's burial service at the cemetery."

"So what does that have to do with your sudden decision to go to Springvale? Honestly, Mother, sometimes your logic is really hard to follow. Mac says something about ghosts and an argument Mr. Bowman can't or won't verify, and this leads to you and Aunt Mary hightailing it to some nursing home. I don't get it."

"Neither did I at first, but after talking to Jason Bowman I got to thinking. What did Harmon and Jason have in common other than the close proximity of their mothers' graves? That's when it dawned on me. Where did both Mrs. Brinker and Mrs. Bowman spend their last years? Not at home, but *in* a home. Maybe the same one that once employed Harrison. The place had to be reasonably close because Jason and Harmon were good sons and would naturally want to visit their mothers as often as possible. If you jump on the interstate, Springvale isn't that far. The information telephone operator was a big help. She

189

looked up various private nursing homes in the area and came up with three: The Asian-American Infirmary, Sacred Heart Sanctuary, and Safe Harbor Women's Home."

"Oh, I get it. Since neither the Bowmans nor the Brinkers were of Asian ancestry, nor were they members of the Catholic faith, Safe Harbor was the logical choice. So the two old ladies were residents in the place where Harrison used to work. That's interesting. And when he left, so did Stella. Am I right?"

Pleased that she was, JR went a bit further. "Maybe what Mac overheard was an argument over Harrison's kissing up to certain residents. Harmon might have suspected that Harrison found playing favorites to be financially rewarding. He probably expected Harrison to either offer restitution or his resignation from Sleepy Hollow. Maybe even both. Instead, they end up arguing about morality. God, Mr. Brinker was always so righteous. Hey, wait a minute, Mom. None of this explains how you knew that Roxy Bloom was Rosalie Blumquist's 'nom de plume.'"

"You mean alias," I corrected. "From what I've seen of Roxy, she's not about to put pen to paper. It's kind of a shame, since she most likely has a bestseller wandering around in that mixed-up brain of hers. Unfortunately, for the book-buying public, working in a library has been the extent of her literary career."

"Whatever," JR retorted, sticking her tongue out at me. "Now, where were we before I was so rudely interrupted? Oh yeah, you were about to reveal how your great powers of logical deduction led to the unmasking of the furtive Rosalie."

"It was easy. I simply asked Mac's ghost for help," I said, matching JR's mischievous grin with one of my own.

"Seriously, when I learned that Safe Harbor's oldest resident has a habit of slipping into the past, insisting that Safe Harbor is a gambling den run by the mob, something clicked in my head. Call it a hunch or good deductive reasoning, but when I called out the name Roxy Bloom, I got a response. After visiting with her, I'm convinced that she's the real deal. The problem is that she drifts in and out of reality, and in between times, she falls asleep. Not your ideal witness but as far as I'm concerned, damn close to it."

Rummaging through the pantry shelves for something to go with my coffee, I found a handful of overlooked peanut butter Kisses. Like the coffee, the candy was stale.

It took a lot of dedicated chewing before I regained the power of speech.

"I only wish I could've visited a bit longer with Roxy. I felt sure that she was just about to name names. It's frustrating not to be able to communicate with three key players in this tangled triangle of murder, mayhem, and mystery."

JR held up three fingers. "Let me guess. First, there's Stella, who's in the intensive care unit and not allowed phone calls or visitors. Could be that she's wrong about her brother being a murder victim. Then, there's the foxy Roxy. Is she really senile, or is it an act? Don't forget, Mother, she's managed to fool a lot of people for a long, long time. And lastly, there's Harmon Brinker, who's dead and buried. And I, for one, hope he stays that way."

"I couldn't agree with you more, kid. The last thing this case needs is another ghost, real or imaginary." I unwrapped another piece of the candy, hoping that it wouldn't be as stale as the first piece. Wrong.

"Hey, Mom, are you as hungry as I am? Pops really should have ordered at least a party-size pizza. A large isn't big enough anymore. The twins ate over half of it, which didn't leave much for the rest of us. Isn't there anything else to snack on besides petrified Halloween candy and diet doggy treats?"

I was trying to unlock my jaws so I could give JR an answer when a smiling Matt arrived with an armload of carry-out from Milano's. Knowing our family's propensity for Italian food, he'd picked up an antipasto tray, cheese-and-garlic breadsticks, freshly baked amaretti, and a pint of creamy spumoni.

Once again, the cottage's kitchen was filled with the aroma of good food, children's laughter, and pleasant conversation. Matt and Charlie made short work of the antipasto, leaving only a few pickled beets and a couple of radishes on the tray. JR and I did a number on the breadsticks while the twins dropped enough macaroon crumbs and chunks of the Italian ice cream to keep Pesty busy for the rest of the evening.

Coffeed out, I'd switched to Charlie's homemade wine. A small glass of the strong, tasty liquid left me feeling warm, sleepy, and totally unprepared for Matt's announcement that Tom MacNulty had been arrested and charged with the murder of Harrison Fowler.

According to Matt, Mac had the motive, means, and opportunity. When the missing medical kit, with its supply of epinephrine, was found smashed in the wastecan under the bar, a warrant was issued with the bartender's name on it.

Matt's announcement, followed by more of the wine, did me in, sending me off to bed, where I immediately fell into a deep sleep. When I awoke in the morning, nothing had changed except that I had one heck of a hangover.

CHAPTER
TWENTY-ONE

Although I've known Luanne Winslow and her parents, Winnie and Cord Stanford, from day one, I'd always considered them to be acquaintances rather than friends, which is why I was surprised to find Luanne on the doorstep of Kettle Cottage the following morning. I forgot my hangover long enough to remember my manners and invite Luanne into the kitchen.

She followed up her acceptance with an explanation for her visit. "Mac told me to come see you. He says that you're the smartest person in town. I hope you can help 'cause nobody else can. My mother says Mac's as guilty as sin. Daddy's convinced that if Mac had asked me to marry him instead of stalling, I wouldn't have run off with Gary. Mother says that Mac never had any intention of marrying me. She says I should have done like Vanessa and found me a rich old man. Mother says Vanessa is going to end up being a rich, young widow."

When Luanne stopped for a breath, I offered her a cup of freshly brewed coffee.

"No thanks. I already had a cup of tea before dropping the baby off at the sitter's house." She frowned as I helped myself to the coffee and a cigarette. "Mother says coffee isn't good for you when you're nursing a baby like I am."

From the look on the girl's face as I puffed away, I knew, without being told, that her mother also said that smoking is hazardous to your health. So far, it was the only thing her mother had said that was entirely truthful.

Luanne's dark eyes showed all the signs of an upcoming crying spell. Her bottom lip began to tremble ever so slightly.

"Mother says the police are right about Mac deliberately adding that peanut stuff to the special seasoning mix. Mother says Mac was jealous because Harrison was dating me. He wasn't jealous, honest, Mrs. Hastings. He knew I only went out with Mr. Fowler to please my parents. Personally, I couldn't stand the man."

With a defiant tilt of her chin, Luanne added, "Besides, he was way too old for me. Golly, Mr. Fowler must have been at least fifty years old, or close to it."

The strong emphasis Luanne placed on the word *fifty* made me wonder if perhaps she believed that Harrison had died of old age.

"Listen Luanne, the last thing I want to do is to come between you and your folks, but you've got to stop quoting your mother. It makes you sound as though you can't think for yourself. I'm sure that your mother would agree," I lied, knowing full well that Winnie Stanford enjoyed imposing her will on her family, especially Luanne. If the girl had been allowed to think for herself, she would have never married Gary Winslow.

"Since you've asked for my advice Luanne, the first thing you should do is to contact Jerry Dobbs in Indianapolis. He is the best criminal attorney in the state of Indiana. When you call his office tell Phyliss, she's Jerry's right-hand girl, that I said Jerry would help. He and I go way back. In fact, he's the closest thing I have to a brother. His mother and mine were best friends. Years ago, when Jerry's parents were killed in an auto accident, he came to live with us. We became his family."

What I didn't tell Luanne was that I was only nine at the time and had a terrific crush on the handsome teenager. When Jerry left for college, my young heart was broken for almost a week. To console me, my father brought home a puppy. The way Jerry likes to tell it, he was replaced by a dog. Jerry was, and still is, a member of my family.

Luanne shoved the attorney's card I'd given her deep into the back pocket of her jeans. "Thanks, and I'm sorry I interrupted your brunch. I hope you get rid of your sinus headache. I guess I'll be going now."

Even though she'd said all the things that people say when they are ready to leave, Luanne didn't move. It was as if her shoes had been nailed to the floor. There was only one thing I could think of that would account for her reluctance — she was holding something back.

"Luanne, dear, what is it that you're not telling me?" My head was throbbing like the jungle drums in a Tarzan movie. I wasn't in any shape to play mind games and it was a struggle not to let it show. I could only imagine what her mother would say about people who consume too much homemade wine.

"Well, you know, Mac thought, like, maybe if you could figure out who the real murder is, then Mother would have to stop saying all those nasty things about him." Blinking back her tears, Luanne made an effort to smile with a mouth that refused to cooperate.

"You see, me and Mac were secretly married on All Saints' Day. We were going to tell everyone, including my parents, but now we can't."

"Why not?" I asked, wondering what the consequences would be if I took two more aspirins. While I was debating the wisdom of doing so, I realized that Luanne was in the middle of answering my question.

". . . and people, especially my parents, would say that he only married me to keep me from testifying against him. If you don't find the real murderer," Luanne sobbed, "I'll never be known as the new Mrs. Mac-Nulty, not ever."

I gave the girl a tissue, a hug, and my word that I would do my best. I also took two more aspirins. Watching Luanne drive away in her new SUV, I wondered if I had taken on more problems, or swallowed more aspirin, than I could handle.

"Jeez, what have I done?" I asked Pesty, who was busy searching the kitchen floor for anything edible. "I should stick to redoing people's homes instead of their lives. Maybe Mac did kill Harrison. Maybe Harrison was mean to Mave."

Hearing the big dog's name, the little Kees

rolled her fur and growled. I was impressed. "See if you can hold that pose while I'm gone. There's a killer loose in Seville, and you, my fuzzy friend, are the only protection I've got."

By the time I'd traded my comfortable sweats for a sweater set and slacks, Pesty was fast asleep under the kitchen table. I locked up the house on my way out. Surely I'd be back before Charlie returned from helping Denny. Hopefully the installation of the store's new overhead door would be an all-day job.

"Hello," I whispered into my cell phone, hoping the jangling tune announcing the incoming call hadn't disrupted the peace and quiet of Seville's public library. But one look at Mrs. Milhower's face told me it had.

The head librarian didn't seem to mind the extra work I'd created for her and the staff. In fact, I had the impression that she enjoyed digging through the old files and making photocopies. The model of discretion, Mrs. Milhower didn't question why I was so interested in old newspaper articles that focused on Grant Higgins's military service, his marriage to Verna, and Finky Dee's death. The woman helped me because I played by her rules and didn't make waves or noise. Now, thanks to Charlie, I was doing both.

"For crissakes, is that you?" Charlie's voice boomed through the phone, bouncing off the marble floor and pillars. "Would you care to explain to me just why in the hell our house is all locked up? I can't get in. Where in God's name are you, anyway? And speak louder. I can hardly hear you."

"Charlie, I'm on my way home. Hang up and don't call me again." Turning the phone off, I apologized to Mrs. Milhower — in a quiet voice, of course.

"I can't thank you enough for all your help. I'm so sorry about the phone call but that's my Charlie. He's such a worrywart." It wasn't the greatest explanation, but it was the best I could do. I paid for the photocopies, thanked Mrs. Milhower again, and rushed out of the library.

The late-afternoon sun had already scooted behind the ridge, leaving only a smudge of orange-red color in the sky. In a few minutes, it would be dark. I'd spent most of the afternoon in the library, and the wealth of information I'd obtained made it worth my time. I now had a pretty good idea that it was Verna Higgins who pumped Finky full of lead and why, but what, if anything, his death had to do with the two recent deaths wasn't clear to me, at least not yet.

I'd already started the van's motor when I spied the folded piece of paper, which someone had obviously placed on the windshield. I considered dislodging the paper with a quick swish of the wipers but thought better of it. If everyone in town did the same, the streets would be littered with notices for the constant yard and garage sales. Lowering the driver's side window, I made a grab for the paper. Since I didn't have time to read it, and with no place to dispose of it, I added the notice to the library file folder. I had enough to do without running around, trying to find treasure among other people's trash.

Traffic was moving, and I would have made the green light at the corner had it not been for the truck in front of me. When the truck made an unexpected stop, I slammed on the brakes and my seat belt lost all of its slack, pinning me to the seat. I could only watch as the folder slid from the passenger seat and spilled its contents on the floor. Like Charlie, the papers would just have to sit and wait. I didn't have time to deal with them now.

An easy-to-fix chicken and rice casserole, followed by his favorite dessert (warm apple pie with a slice of cheese), and Charlie was back to being his old, charming self. He even loaded the dishwasher and fed the dog while I relaxed with an Irish coffee and a cigarette. When I told him where I'd been, Charlie believed the visit to be design-related, and that was fine with me since I hadn't prepared any cover story.

With Charlie snoozing in front of the television, I decided it was the opportune time for me to review the information I'd gotten from the library files. However, first I had to retrieve the folder and papers from the floor of the van.

A peek through the kitchen curtains confirmed what I already knew — it was a very dark night. Not wanting to venture out alone, I turned to Pesty and suggested that perhaps she would like to accompany me. She responded by retreating to the den, where she curled up on the sofa for a nap.

Like its modern descendant, the prehistoric Kees reveled in the warmth of a fire, scheduled meals, and the great indoors. Proof of this has been found in the Neanderthal pictographs recently discovered on the inside walls of cave dwellings. Not particularly imaginative, Neanderthals tended to draw what they saw, and what they saw was an overfed, cavebound, lounging Keeshond.

Experts claim that the images depict the woolly bison, but as a Kees owner, I beg to differ with them.

With my chances almost nil of encountering a saber-toothed tabby, or a humming-bird the size of the Goodyear blimp, I said a quick prayer, stepped outside, and was immediately eveloped in darkness. Moving cautiously along the drive, I told myself it was the cold wind, not the presence of some evil force, that was giving me goose bumps.

I was almost to where I'd parked the van when the sound of voices drifted over the tall, thick hedge that separates our property from the Birdwells'. I recognized Billy's voice immediately, and it took me only a microsecond longer to do the same with Tammie's.

"I can't believe that the cops think Mac killed Fowler," said Billy. "So what if he didn't like the guy very much. That doesn't prove anything. Shoot, almost everybody, except maybe Vanessa Higgins, didn't like him and that includes me and you. I can see Mac taking a poke at him for putting the moves on Luanne, but murder? No way."

"Well, maybe he just snapped, you know, like Romeo did when he couldn't have Juliet."

"Tammie, if that was the case, Mac would be in the morgue, not jail," Billy replied with a small chuckle.

"Oh, I suppose you're right. Lordy, he must have really loved her to do something so drastic."

At this point, I wasn't sure which pair of star-crossed lovers were being discussed — Romeo and Juliet or Mac and Luanne? Apparently, neither did Billy, who promptly changed the subject.

"I went over to the hospital today to see Stella but some purple-haired wacko running the visitors' desk stopped me. She said Doctor Parker won't let anyone, not even Matt Cusak, in Stella's room." Billy then murmured something I didn't catch. What followed was the sound of a passionate, goodnight kiss.

With his shock of flaming red hair, toothy smile, and liberal sprinkling of freckles, the former high-school football hero seemed more like an all-American boy than someone's lover or sex symbol. I felt kind of cheesy eavesdropping on Billy Birdwell and the current object of his affection. Like a deadbeat renter, I waited for my chance to slip away. It came when I heard Tammie start her car and the Birdwells' front door close.

Resuming my trek, I wished that I'd purchased one of those handy dandy flashlights, which, according to the late-night television advertisement, could very well save my life. Without it, I stumbled along until I literally bumped into the van.

The interior light failed to come on when I opened the van's door, leaving me to search in the pitch dark. Gingerly, I poked around the floor of the vehicle until I found the folder and its spilled contents. After stuffing the papers in the folder and locking the van, I threw caution to the wind and made a dash for my well-lit kitchen.

"No, there's nothing in it for you," I quietly assured Pesty, who had returned to the kitchen once she realized that a sleeping Charlie offered nothing in the way of protection or food. "See," I said, grabbing the yard sale notice from the folder and waving it under her nose, "this is for me, not you, my fainthearted friend." And indeed, it was.

The message was printed in black crayon on white paper. Other than some oily smudges along the fold lines, the paper was quite ordinary and unlike its message, which was anything but: MIND YOUR OWN BUSINESS BITCH OR DIE!!!

A sleepless night, followed by a worrisome day, brought me to the conclusion that the note was a threat and nothing more than a threat. Tucking the nasty note in my purse for safekeeping, I decided not to tell my family about the incident as it would've alarmed Charlie, worried JR, and infuriated Matt. I also had decided that until I had some feedback from Horatio Bordeaux, who was still in the process of finding some information for me, my investigation was on hold.

In the meantime, the promise I'd made to the twins took preference over everything: The three of us were going to celebrate Veterans Day in Indianapolis. Our plans included a visit to the famed Children's Museum, a stop at Monument Circle for the ceremonies, and lunch at Pufferbelly's, downtown Indy's newest and hottest, family-friendly restaurant.

CHAPTER TWENTY-TWO

It was a spectacular, golden autumn morning when I arrived at the Cusaks' refurbished, 1920s-style bungalow. Within minutes, the twins were out of the house and in the backseat of the van. Buckling up, they waved goodbye to JR and Matt. The kids were happy to be going, and from the look on their faces, the parents were happy to see them go. Before driving off, I gave JR my word that we would return no earlier than three in the afternoon and no later than six in the evening.

Our first stop was the museum. I watched as Kerry and Kelly doggedly searched for ancient artifacts at the cleverly fabricated Egyptian site. Because it was a school holiday, the place was crowded, which didn't surprise me. But I was surprised that it didn't take bribery, threats, or a court order to get the twins to quit the dig.

"When I grow up, I'm going to be an

archaeologist," Kerry announced proudly as we drove into one of downtown Indianapolis' multilevel, indoor parking facilities.

"Oh, no, you're not. I picked it first," said an annoyed Kelly. "Last month when Grandpa took us to the zoo, you said you wanted to be a zoologist, so that's what you have to be. I'm tellin' Grandpa on you."

At eight years of age, Kelly was the spitting image of his father. Kerry, on the other hand, looked and acted so much like her mother, that it was like watching JR grow up all over again.

"Go ahead; see if I care. I can change my mind if I want to. Mama says girls get to do that 'cause we've got some kind of special privilege that boys don't have. So there." Kerry's heart-shaped face was a study in pure, gender satisfaction.

"Well, I got dibs on Egypt. I called it first, so there yourself," Kelly shot back with a finality that his sister was not about to accept.

The argument over occupations and locations intensified as I drove from level to level looking for an empty space not reserved for the handicapped. The twins continued to bicker even after I'd finally parked the van and was shepherding them toward the elevator. We had only a few yards to go when I heard the screeching tires of a speeding vehicle.

Acting on instinct, I pushed the twins out of the way as it sped by. The vehicle cut so close to me it clipped the purse I was carrying. The impact sent the leather tote flying in the air, scattering its contents over the pavement.

Ordering the kids to stay between the parked cars, I began picking up what I could find of my belongings, all the while cursing the fact that I hadn't gotten a good look at the driver or the vehicle. I thought it might have been a large station wagon, but Kelly swore it had been a van. Kerry was equally sure that it was a luxury SUV, "you know Grandma, like the kind Mr. Stanford sells." A further disagreement erupted regarding the driver's identity. Kelly insisted that it'd been a woman behind the wheel, and Kerry said she saw a man. None of us agreed on the vehicle's color.

"Okay, okay. Let's not argue about it. I'm just happy that nobody got hurt, so forget it," I said, not wanting to alarm the twins by dwelling on the close call.

We arrived at Monument Circle in time to hear the mayor's speech on the sacrifices made by past and present members of the armed forces. The presence of uniformed veterans, flags, and the military band filled the twins with so much patriotism that I was pretty sure the garage incident had been forgotten.

During the short walk to the restaurant in Circle Center, an enclosed multilevel mall, the twins argued over which military branch was the bravest. I was beginning to understand why Matt and JR had looked so happy to see us pull out of the driveway that morning.

Pufferbelly's was jammed. We would have to wait if we wanted to sit together at the long, winding counter where elegant, oversized toy trains thundered by as they made their way to and from the kitchen. The trains stopped to pick up orders and to make deliveries of food to hungry customers. The servers, outfitted in coveralls, engineer caps, and red bandannas, assisted in the unloading of hamburgers, hot dogs, fries, and soft drinks. Desserts (huge chocolate-coated, ice cream bonbons), arrived in bright red, refrigerated box cars.

The limited menu is designed to keep things moving, on schedule, and to insure a fast turnover, but kids of all ages like the place so much that hardly anyone eats and runs.

The long wait was worth it. Pufferbelly's

was a new experience for the twins. They were truly excited, giving the restaurant two thumbs-up even before they'd tasted any of the food. Of course, our order included dessert. When the shiny refrigerated car came to a halt at our station, I slid open the double doors and removed the plate of bonbons. Along with the ordered desserts was a lone, Chinese fortune cookie. It looked more than a bit out of place.

"When did Pufferbelly's add the cookies to the menu?" I asked the nearest server who was busy unloading two flatbed cars of food for a family of five — mother, father, and three lively little boys. The rambunctious trio had put their daddy's wallet on a passing train. To the boys' disappointment, the yard-man (an agile, assistant manager), retrieved the item before any harm was done.

"It didn't," answered the frazzled woman without looking my way. "If you got one, somebody down the line probably stuck it in the boxcar; you know, like some kids will do. If I was you, lady, I'd just toss it."

"Aren't you gonna read your fortune, Grandma?" Kelly asked, popping an entire bonbon in his mouth. That the kid had room for dessert amazed me. He had already downed three hot dogs with the works, a double order of cheese-topped fries, and a couple of root beers. The boy may look like a Cusak, but he has the appetite of a Hastings.

"Now Grandma," Kerry said, taking a dainty bite of the ice cream delicacy while ignoring the half-eaten hamburger and the untouched, small order of fries on her plate, "you really should read it. It might be important."

Faster than you can say product tampering, I opened the cookie and read the fortune: REST IN PEACE.

I glanced around the crowded restaurant. No one looked familiar, sinister, or out of place. Perhaps the server was right about it being someone's idea of a joke. I thought it best to shrug the matter off since I didn't want to upset the twins. I hated to think about what Matt would say if he got wind of the cookie or the garage incident. The less said the better it would be for all concerned.

"What did it say?" demanded the twins in unison. "Is this your lucky day, Grandma?" Kerry wanted to know.

"Any day with you two kids is my lucky day." With a forced smile, I crumpled the cookie, and the fortune, in my napkin. Then to the twins' delight and surprise, I popped the remaining bonbon in my mouth. It was delicious.

On the trip home, the twins argued over who had had the most fun that day. I ignored them and used the time to rethink my decision to put the investigation on hold. Like Kerry, I could exercise that special privilege and change my mind. Rather than frighten me away, the events of the day made me more determined than ever to solve the mysteries. I was back on the case, Horatio or no Horatio.

JR was on hand to greet us as the twins tumbled from the van and scrambled onto the porch. Snatching the junior engineer cap from Kelly's head, and the red bandanna from Kerry's ponytail (Pufferbelly's doesn't miss a merchandising trick), JR quizzed the twins on their behavior.

"I hope you two remembered what your father told you about your constant bickering. You didn't argue today, did you?"

For the first time since I'd picked them up, the twins were at a loss for words. I came to their rescue and assured JR that the kids were as good as gold and hadn't had a single disagreement the entire time they were with me. I was rewarded with a double dose of heartfelt hugs, kisses, and thank-yous from my grandchildren.

"Well, that's nice to hear for a change. You two get inside and wash your hands. Kelly, it's your turn to feed the dog and the fish. Kerry, you get to feed the cat and the turtle. Daddy already fed the hamsters and the parakeet."

JR waited until the twins were in the house and out of earshot before saying anything more.

"Okay, Mom, let's have it, and I want the truth. What the hell's been going on?"

"Oh for heaven's sake, so I fibbed about the kids fighting. Big deal. That's part of being a grandmother." I found it annoying that my daughter was making much ado about nothing.

JR tried again. The second time she was more specific. "I'm not talking about that. I'm talking about Winnie Stanford. She was at your house this morning looking for you. Pops sent her over here. She came tearing up the drive in her big station wagon right after you pulled away."

"You're kidding," I said, knowing that she wasn't. "I wonder what Winnie Stanford wanted to see me about. You know, I'll bet she has some decorating dilemma. Yeah, that's it. She's got a design problem."

"Nice try, Mother. When I told her you were spending the day in Indy with the twins and I didn't know when you'd be home, she beat a fast retreat, but not before telling Matt that if anything happens to Luanne, she's holding you and Uncle Jerry personally responsible. Come on, Mother, talk."

Having no choice, I gave JR an edited version of Luanne's visit. I purposely left out much of what I believed had been told to me in confidence.

"Well, then," huffed JR, "Mrs. Stanford's the one who should mind her own business. Everyone, even an accused murderer, has the right to an attorney. All you did was to give Luanne some asked-for advice. I'm telling you, Mom, that woman is scary. I wouldn't put anything past her."

I turned down JR's offer of fresh apple cider and homemade doughnuts, and headed straight for Kettle Cottage, a hot cup of coffee, and a cigarette. I dearly missed all three. It had been a long and exhausting day.

CHAPTER
TWENTY-THREE

The following afternoon, once lunch was out of the way and Charlie was busy getting the yard ready for the coming winter, I telephoned Mary. One ring, two rings, three rings. On the fourth ring, Mary's voice mixed with the recorded voice-mail message until she triumphed over technology.

"Hello. Oh my stars, wait a minute. I think I have to reset this thing. Oops, wrong button. Okay, go ahead, caller," Mary said, sounding every bit like the long-distance operator she'd once been. Mary had worked for Ma Bell in the days when it was the first and last word in telephone service.

"Mary, it's me, Jean. I'm promoting a new cause and I could use your help."

"Okay," she chirped. "What's the cause? I hope it has something to do with helping the poor or homeless. I'm getting kind of burned out protecting animal rights, saving the environment, and counseling alien ab-ductees. Although, I do have to say that I've heard some almost unbelievable stories. Did you know Herbie Waddlemeyer has been examined by extraterrestials more than a dozen times? And aboard their ship, no less. Lately, they've been taking him right out of his own bed."

"How convenient," I replied quickly, anxious to get back on track. "What would you say if I told you that we'll be going to VanVern Manor to promote a charity gem show?"

"I'd say you're out of your mind. Neither one of them strikes me as being athletic. Vern gave up golf years ago, and Vanessa doesn't even clean the house. She's got a full-time, live-in maid. I don't think they would be interested in any kind of gymnas-tics event."

"Jeez, I said gem like in diamonds, not gym like in physical activity. Besides, the whole charity thing is a sham. It's an excuse to get the two of them to sit down and talk to me. I need you to be my witness. Now, are you coming with me, or not?"

"My stars, you certainly go from nice to crabby awfully fast. You could've told me that we were going sleuthing."

I was about to correct her, but thought

the better of it. The idea that we might be digging up some unwanted ghost from the past would have only set her off. Mary is a true believer in the unexplained.

"Give me five minutes, Gin. I'll be ready." The excitement in her voice was unmistakable. For both our sakes, I hoped that I wasn't getting us in over our heads.

Without giving notice, the colors of autumn had faded away. A wall of thick, gray clouds had formed a protective shell over the sun, preventing even the strongest of rays from making an appearance. Everything at ground level seemed to be the color of mud, or coated with the mucky stuff, thanks to the previous night's rain. Against this dreary backdrop, the old Higgins house looked far from inviting as Mary and I made our way up the brick walk toward the wraparound front porch.

"Did you see that?" Mary demanded, tugging on the sleeve of my cream-colored wool pullover. I'd purchased the sweater in Dublin, Ireland, where Charlie and I had celebrated our thirty-fifth wedding anniversary. To say that I treasure the sweater would be an understatement.

"Jeez, take it easy on the goods, Mar. Another yank like that and this hunk of imported wool is going to end up looking more like a fisherman's net than his sweater." I gave up trying to reshape the sagging sleeve.

"I'm sorry, Gin. I thought I saw something watching us from the little thingy way up there." Mary pointed to a tiny, beveled-glass turret window. "It didn't move away; it faded away, you know, like it wasn't real, or of this earth. I'll bet it was some kind of omen. Maybe it was trying to warn us to turn back before it's too late."

"Well, don't worry about it. It's not like we're Hansel and Gretel. What's so bad about being watched by a transparent specter, anyway? If Herbie Waddlemeyer had a choice, he'd probably pick seeing a ghost once in awhile over nightly visits from a bunch of Martian proctologists."

I thought what I said would get a laugh out of Mary. Instead, she solemnly agreed with me.

"I suppose you're right. I imagine Herbie would welcome the change, especially after all he's been through. He hardly ever sleeps anymore."

Crossing the porch, we stood side by side in front of the ornately framed entrance. I was ready to give the bell pull a good tug when the solid oak door unexpectedly swung open, bringing us face to face with the lord of the manor, Vernon Garrison Higgins.

"And what, may I ask, brings two of Seville's loveliest to my humble doorstep?" Wearing a paisley-print silk smoking jacket, a smooth, white satin ascot, charcoal-gray flannel slacks, and shiny, black tasseled loafers Vernon Higgins looked and acted the part of the wealthy, old lecher. He reeked of alcohol and stale cigars. His hooded, dark eyes swept over me before zeroing in on the unsuspecting Mary.

With a reputation for groping well-endowed females, he was about to make a chest-high lunge for my well-endowed sister-in-law when the air crackled with the sounds of a familiar, overused, Southern accent.

"Vernon, honey, are y'all goin' to ask them to step in or what? And stop blockin' the doorway like an over-the-hill bouncer. Y'all know what Ah'm sayin'?"

As was her habit, the lady of the house was dressed to the nines. Her taste in daywear was impeccable. The beige-and-black wool sheath dress was the perfect backdrop for the stunning display of expensive gold jewelry. Surprisingly, she wore little, if any, makeup. Perhaps to compensate for this shortfall, she had drenched herself in an

221

overpowering, expensive-smelling perfume. The scent was vaguely familiar.

We were led into the formal parlor. It still looked impressive in spite of Vanessa's newest acquisition: a mawkish oil painting depicting a postmortem Elvis surrounded by a celestial chorus. When we'd been seated, we were offered drinks by our host and coffee by our hostess. Vanessa dispatched her slightly tipsy husband to the kitchen with orders not to make the coffee too weak or too strong.

With Vern safely out of the room, I double-talked my way through a presentation for the nonexistent charity event. By the time he returned, I had Vanessa talking up a storm about her collection of baubles, bangles, and beads. The collection included some old and distinctive pieces that had once belonged to her husband's late mother, Verna Seville Higgins.

"Oh how marvelous for you," I gushed, "to think you've actually handled these treasures. I've only seen them in old photographs such as the one depicting Verna and Grant celebrating his release from the hospital. He'd been seriously wounded during the Meuse-Argonne offensive. Verna wore a ruby brooch for the occasion. Of course, I'm not telling you anything you don't already know."

Although she tried to hide it, I could tell that Vanessa was hearing all of this for the first time. She was clearly intrigued.

"And there's that terrific engagement photo. You know the one I mean, Vanessa. It's the one showing Verna wearing the huge, sapphire ring. The copy stated that the color of the blue stone matched Grant's eyes as well as Verna's. I think that's so sweet, don't you?" Vanessa nodded her head.

Catching the tail end of the conversation, Vernon Higgins blanched visibly. With shaking hands, he set the silver tray with the coffee and such on a nearby, mahogany sideboard.

"I'm not feeling all that well, so if you ladies will excuse me, I think I'll go upstairs and rest a while."

"Y'all do no such thing," squawked his wife, "we've got company and it's the maid's day off. Y'all serve that coffee and get yourself a cup, too."

Turning her attention away from her husband, Vanessa attempted to resume our conversation. "How in the world did y'all come across pitchers of Vernon's kinfolk?" Not waiting for an answer she rushed on, "Ah know what. Y'all been snoopin' in that dusty storeroom up at the club like ma husband. He swears it's plum full of stuff like what's hangin' up in the bar. If Vernon ain't pokin' 'round in there, he's up at the cemetery visitin' family. Now, that's downright spooky, y'all know what Ah'm sayin'?"

"Really," I said, trying to remain calm. Unknowingly, Vanessa verified what I'd suspected. "I got my information from the library. It has everything from articles on genetics to old newspaper stories and photographs. It's all there for the asking, so I did." My words were meant for Vern Higgins, who was in the process of adding crushed ice to a silver-plated cocktail shaker. "For a small fee," I continued, "you can get copies of almost anything and I do mean anything."

An uneasy quiet settled over the four of us until it was broken by a snorting giggle. "Oh my stars, I didn't know that was going to pop out of me." Embarrassed, Mary nearly dropped the foil-wrapped candy she'd taken from the crystal dish that Vernon had placed in front of her.

"Okay, Mrs. Hastings," Vern Higgins demanded, narrowing his brown eyes, "how much do you want? Before you answer, I should remind you what happened to the last person who was blackmailing me."

"Blackmail?" screeched Vanessa, jumping

up from the celery-green sofa and spilling coffee on its damask upholstery. "Damn you, Vernon Higgins, y'all killed Harrison cause he was a blackmailer? And here Ah thought it was 'cause y'all was crazy jealous over him and me."

"Vanessa, shut up," he said, not bothering to hide his anger. Treating her as if she were a naughty child, he ordered his young wife to leave the room. "You heard me, get out."

"Well, Ah never!" Vanessa screamed in Vernon's bloated face, her own contorted in rage. She was standing close enough to be engulfed in her husband's gin-laced breath.

"Yes, you have, Vanessa dear. Harrison wasn't the first and most likely, won't be the last." Pouring the contents of the shaker into his waiting glass, Vern held the cocktail high in the air. He looked like a native shaman offering a sacrifice to the gods. "Care to join me, my pet? A martini goes well with humble pie, or so I've heard."

For a fraction of a second Vanessa wavered before fleeing the room, only stopping long enough to snatch a decorative figurine from the top of the sewing table. She hurled the bauble at the marble fireplace mantel. Upon impact, shards of Austrian crystal skittered across the hardwood floor. If Vanessa thought the rash act would elicit some emotion from her husband, be it shock or remorse, she was wrong.

Shrugging his shoulders, Vern Higgins took a large swig of the refused offering. He ignored the squeaking crunch of broken bric-a-brac under his shoes and sat down heavily in the green-leather Stickley chair, drink in hand. "Now where were we? Oh yes, we were about to enter into negotiations. Tell me, Mrs. Hastings, do you want cash like your predecessor, or will you take a check?"

"Come now, Mr. Higgins, I'm no more a blackmailer than you are a murderer. The only crime you've committed is entering cemetery grounds after hours, a misdemeanor at best. Scaring Tom MacNulty half to death with your unorthodox behavior in the club was stupid, not criminal. Apparently, you thought the blackmailer's source of information came from Sleepy Hollow's large collection of World War I memorabilia, some of which is on display in the bar."

"You mean he's the ghost? Wait a minute," said Mary as she looked longingly at the foil-wrapped candy, "I'm getting awfully confused. Who was blackmailing who and why? By the way Mr. Higgins, the truffles are delicious. I'll have one more, that is if you don't mind. Where on earth did you get them? Not locally, I presume."

"Help yourself, dear lady. They're from Marshall Field's in Chicago. It's nice to see someone enjoying them. Vanessa rarely touches them. Like most young women of today, she worries about her weight, although I don't know why. She's already reached her goal in life, which was to marry a rich, old man who forgives and forgets."

"Yes. Had the blackmailer threatened to expose Vannesa's affair with Harrison Fowler, you probably wouldn't have paid. Protecting your wife's reputation has never been a priority. Am I correct so far?" I asked as Mary reached for yet another chocolate truffle.

Finishing what was left of his drink, Vern Higgins nodded his head in affirmation. "I could have dealt with Vanessa's infidelity. I've strayed a time or two myself."

He waited a moment before speaking again. "When I realized the blackmailer was threatening to reveal certain Higgins family secrets, I paid. May I ask what you're going to do with the information, if, as you claim, you're not a blackmailer?"

With her mouth full of chocolate, Mary came to my defense. "Na shee har Misher Higuns, Misha Hashin ish na bacmaler. Shes jush slooshing, rah Shin?"

"What Mrs. England is trying to say is that I'm not here to blackmail anyone. I came here to expose a ghost and solve an old mystery." I was tempted to add that the two of them, one a chocoholic and the other an alcoholic, weren't making things easy for me. Pressing on, I informed our host that if the authorities knew the purpose of his late-night visits to the cemetery was to leave the payoff money on his father's tombstone, he wouldn't be charged with trespassing, or anything else. The grave's isolated location made it the perfect site for the drop.

"You're not the villain in all this," I reminded him, "you're the victim, or at least, one of them."

"Jean, dear," said Mary in her best tsk-tsk manner between bites of chocolate, "don't say tombstone or grave. It sounds so dated. Now days, people refer to such things as markers and plots. Besides, everyone knows that Grant Higgins is buried in the Seville family's mausoleum."

I couldn't trust myself to look at Mary. "You'll have to excuse Mrs. England. She often finds herself in the right church but in the wrong pew."

"Congratulations, Mrs. Hastings," said Vern, "you've done your homework. You know then, the war injury rendered him incapable of fathering a child. I'm not sure Mother was fully aware of this when they married. It was a time when infertility was, more often than not, blamed on the woman."

Vern poured himself another drink as Mary reached for a truffle. The cocktail shaker and the candy dish, like baskets from the parable of the loaves and fishes, seemed to be bottomless; nevertheless, I persevered.

"As I see it, nothing would be gained by revealing your mother's brief walk on the wild side," I said. "Your father, Francis Dertz, paid for it with his life, and your mother, Verna, paid for shooting him every time she looked into your dark brown eyes. She, too, was married to a man who could forgive and forget. At this late date, I believe that it is the wisest course for all to follow."

"Thank you, Mrs. Hastings. You're as compassionate as you are competent. A true friend. Too bad Vanessa never took a liking to you. She might have learned to be a real lady." With that said, the lord of the manor went from slurping to snoring in the blink of an eye.

"Come on, Mar, let's get out of here." I had a sudden desire for some fresh air. And a cigarette.

Instead of following my lead, Mary went

over to the now-sleeping Vern. Removing the empty glass from his hand, she placed it on the foil-festooned tray.

"Do you think he'll be all right? Should I go see if I can find Vanessa? Or maybe you can do that, Gin, while I take this stuff to the kitchen."

"Yes, no, and leave the damn tray where it is," I ordered, pushing Mary from the room and out the front door.

"I have a feeling the ugly scene we witnessed between those two is actually the tie that binds. Everything has its price, and I think the husband, like the wife, is more than willing to pay the cost. Nothing says sorry like a diamond bracelet, or a mink coat. I'm sure Vanessa will forgive him and accept his peace offering. They deserve each other."

Mary mulled over my words while I concentrated on backing the van down the narrow driveway. Reaching in the bulging pocket of her jacket, she pulled out a truffle.

"Money can't buy happiness, that's for damn sure," Mary declared, expertly peeling the gold foil from the purloined confection before chomping down on the sweet, "but it sure can buy some mighty fine chocolate. What?" she exclaimed, her round, blue eyes testifying to her innate innocence.

"You heard the man. He said I should help myself."

I was anxious to get Mary home. I had things to do and places to go, the first of which was to stop at Horatio's and pick up the report.

CHAPTER
TWENTY-FOUR

Pesty was beside herself with joy when I finally arrived home. Her food and water bowls were empty, a situation that she found intolerable. Before seeing to her needs, I read the note that Charlie had left on the counter explaining his absence. Apparently, England's new overhead door, like Uncle Fortesque's bed, had developed a mind of its own and was in dire need of adjustment. A postscript to Charlie's note included the promise of Chinese carry-out and a bottle of wine.

I was locked in battle with a new, easy-to-open bag of dog food when the telephone began to ring, causing the frustrated Kees to bark in protest. She wasn't about to allow this intrusion to take preference over her mealtime demands.

"Oh, what the hell," I reasoned aloud, attacking the permanently sealed package with a steak knife, thus spewing dog food all over the kitchen, "let the answering machine take the message. It's the dinner hour so it's a pretty safe bet that it's a telemarketing call." If she had hands, Pesty would have applauded.

I filled Pesty's dish with a measured portion of the ersatz meatballs. Once that was done, I sat down at the kitchen table for a second reading of Horatio's report. Unlike the first reading, which was a shared experience with my son-in-law, this time I had the report, or at least a copy of it, all to myself.

It was close to eight o'clock when Charlie arrived home with the promised food. When all the little white cardboard cartons were empty and our stomachs full, I suggested that we finish our wine in the comfort of the family room.

Charlie readily agreed. "I'll get a fire going; that is if you don't mind if I use one of those paper logs. Otherwise, one of us has to bring in a load of wood from the side yard, and it's not going to be me. I'm really beat."

Since I wasn't about to volunteer, and I could see how tired he was, I told my husband that a paper log fire was fine with me. Had I known that in addition to working on the new door, he'd also helped Denny rearrange stacks of box springs and mattress sets, I would've better understood where he was coming from. Like his twin sister, Mary, Charlie is a friend indeed to those in need.

Sipping our wine, we cuddled in front of the fire like a couple of teenagers, minus the raging hormones, and enjoyed the moment. Pesty was enjoying it, too. She had the sofa all to herself.

"This is nice," my husband murmured softly in my ear. "You know something Jean, we don't spend enough time together. Lately, I've been busy doing my thing, and you've been off somewhere doing yours. By the way, what have you been doing? Denny says you've damn near run poor Mary ragged. He phoned home before we locked up the store, and would you believe Mary turned down his offer to bring home dinner. She said she was too tired to eat."

"Too full would be more like it," I countered. "If she was too tired, it must have been from unwrapping so many Marshall Field's chocolate truffles."

"Chocolate truffles? From Field's? Don't tell me you two drove all the way to Chicago just to get some candy? Ha, ha, ha. Wait 'til I tell Denny." Charlie was laughing so hard, he almost spilled the last swallow of merlot from his glass.

"Denny was worried that you were playing detective again. From past experience, we know how dangerous that can be. But a candy run to Chicago? That's great. In fact, it's downright funny." To my chagrin, Charlie continued to laugh.

"Dangerous? Like how, chum? If you're referring to Ida Sprigg's nephew holding me hostage 'til Matt got the drop on him, I wasn't in danger. He said he wouldn't hurt me," I lied.

The paper log fire had burned itself out. Getting up from the pillows we'd piled on the floor in front of the fireplace, I turned on the night-light, collected the empty wineglasses, and headed for the kitchen. A chuckling Charlie followed close on my heels.

"If and when you get yourself under control, I'll tell you what I really did today," I said, "and believe me, it wasn't driving down the highway stuffing my face with truffles or anything else that would strike you as being funny."

Charlie lightly kissed the back of my neck and locked his arms around my waist. "Okay, sweetheart, I'm ready."

I knew what Charlie was ready for, and it would have to wait. Slipping out of his embrace, I pressed the Play button on the answering machine. There were only three messages: a wrong number, a Mrs. Frawley inquiring if Designer Jeans carried plus sizes, and Jolee Rodgers consenting to my earlier phone request for a second meeting. She left instructions that I was to be in her office by nine-thirty the following morning.

"Jeez, I forgot to get the van's oil changed. I'll have to bring it into Stanford Motors the first thing tomorrow morning before driving to Springvale." Any other time I would've asked Charlie to lend me his car, but it was crucial that I be seen driving my own vehicle. Thinking about the full day ahead and what I hoped to accomplish, I announced to my husband that it was time for bed.

Charlie smiled and pulled me close. "Sweetheart, you sure had me fooled. For a while there, I didn't think we were even on the same page."

One of the advantages of marrying some-one who's both your lover and confidant is that after the lovemaking, you can engage in meaningful conversation. At least, that's how it's supposed to work.

Nestled in Charlie's arms, I brought him up to date on what I'd uncovered about murder, blackmail, and Seville's first family. I told him what had transpired after I'd

236

picked up the report from Horatio, explaining in great detail the next day's game plan that had been worked out by Matt and company.

"Do you think it's too risky?" I asked, expecting kudos for my sleuthing abilities and concern for my safety. Instead, what I got was a low droning noise interspersed with a series of short snorts. Charlie had fallen asleep.

"Thanks a lot, Prince Charming." Making no effort to be gentle or quiet, I grabbed more than my fair share of the down-filled comforter and moved to the far side of the bed. "First it was Roxy, then Vern Higgins, and now my own husband. Maybe I should forget about anaphylaxis and concentrate on narcolepsy."

Feeling a draft on his bare back when he rolled over, Charlie sleepily groped for the missing cover. "Huh? Whaja say, hon?"

"Nothing of importance, dear. I was just wondering if it was as good for you as it was for me. Go back to sleep, Charlie."

Unlike my husband, I was wide awake and spent the next hour tossing and turning. Reluctantly, I threw back the covers, grabbed my robe, and headed downstairs to the kitchen where I helped myself to a glass of cold milk. I thought of warming the milk, then changed my mind. Warm milk only worked in the movies. This was real, not reel life.

I was in the process of making an open-faced peanut butter sandwich to go with the milk when the phone rang. The caller was my friend Horatio Bordeaux.

"Did I wake you? If so, I'm sorry. Jean, we need to talk. Mrs. Daggert told me that you picked up the report, including the extra copy. I was a little apprehensive about leaving the file in her care, but I had to keep my speaking engagement at Garrison General's diabetes seminar. I knew that you would understand, and even though she's a bit bizarre, Mrs. Daggert is generally reliable and very trustworthy."

"Horatio, your housekeeper is more than a bit bizarre. Today, she claimed to be the Oracle of Delphi. She wanted to give me a special reading. I was in such a hurry to leave that I forgot to ask her to relay my thanks to you for all your help. I hope you can forgive me."

"Oh, for heaven's sake, of course I do. Once you get the bill for my services, you might not feel so apologetic. Now, let's get to what I really called about. After locating the information you requested, I took the liberty of contacting an old friend of mine.

He's a profiler for the Bureau. We had an in-depth discussion regarding the subject's personality and propensity for violence."

Horatio stopped to catch his breath. That his breathing sounded so labored worried me, yet I knew better than to interrupt him and inquire about his health.

"I have to tell you Jeannie, I totally agree with him. Your subject is a very sick human being and nobody to mess with. Don't you think it's time to let the authorities take over? You've gone about as far as it's safe for you to go."

I assured my friend that I had no intention of playing a lone hand. We decided that when everything was settled, the two of us would celebrate with one of Mrs. Daggert's famous pot roast dinners complete with roasted potatoes, glazed baby carrots, and baking powder biscuits. I offered to bring a bottle of great, nonalcoholic wine. Then, over a dessert of fruit and cheese, the case would be discussed in full detail.

Thanking him again for the great job he'd done and for his genuine concern, I said good night and hung up the phone.

No longer hungry, I tossed the unfinished sandwich in Pesty's food bowl. Changing my mind, I warmed the milk in the microwave oven and hoped that Hollywood had it right. It did. Five minutes later, I was fast asleep in bed.

CHAPTER
TWENTY-FIVE

A light morning frost clung precariously to the windshield of the van. But, one pass of the wiper blades cleared away the first tangible sign of the coming winter.

With the knob of the van's broken heater in my hand, I debated the pros and cons of returning to the house and exchanging the stylish sweater coat I'd chosen for the less fashionable, albeit warmer, old car coat hanging in the hall closet. I was still undecided when Charlie knocked on the driver's side of the van.

"Hey open up, I've got something for you," he yelled over the din of the motor while pointing to the tall, aluminum mug of steaming coffee he was holding. I knew he felt bad about dozing off the previous night although he swore he had heard most of what I'd said. The coffee was his way of making amends.

White puffs of breath escaped from Charlie's mouth as he stood shivering in the cold morning air. Clad only in a short and threadbare, faded flannel robe, and mismatched slipper socks, he was a sight to behold — a truly charming prince of a fellow.

Rolling down the window, I gratefully accepted the mug and thanked Charlie for his thoughtfulness. I'd overslept and was running late. Although I had managed to wolf down a doughnut while slapping on a modicum of makeup, I'd run out of time to make some badly needed coffee. It had taken me longer than usual to pick out what I was going to wear. Because of what had been planned for the day, it was imperative that my clothing be comfortable and appropriate.

I'd finally settled on a pair of well-worn blue jeans, a generously cut cream-colored, French terry pullover, and my sturdy, brushed suede boots. A newly purchased navy, beige, and gray sweater coat completed my outfit.

A quick kiss on the cheek, followed by my word of honor to Charlie that I would be careful, and I was on my way.

One of the nicest things about a small town is the scarcity of traffic jams. Generally, the traffic in Seville is light and flows smoothly except when the school buses are running their routes, or when some huge piece of farm equipment lumbers through the main thoroughfare, blocking more than one lane.

Like every other town or city in the United States, Seville has its share of social problems, but road rage is definitely not one of them. The short trip across town to Stanford's Service Center was virtually nonstop and hassle-free.

I was in luck. Morty Butterworth, the service manager for Stanford Motors, opened the garage doors and signaled to me to pull the van inside. I would be the first customer of the day, making the prospect of a quick oil change more than likely.

Leaving the keys in the ignition, I took my purse and mug of coffee and proceeded to the customer lounge, where I settled down on a lumpy orange-colored vinyl settee. A stack of old magazines perched perilously on the edge of a wobbly, faux walnut end table. The lone, overhead fluorescent bulb blinked intermittently, making it difficult to read or watch TV, the only two diversions available. In the far corner, an ancient vending machine rattled loudly before letting out an occasional belch. The room's only redeeming feature, as far as I was concerned, was the absence of a NO SMOKING sign. However, I shelved the idea of having a cigarette when a search of the premises failed to produce an ashtray.

The yellow-painted concrete floor showed signs of recent smoking activity. Numerous burn marks marred its surface, which was littered with cigarette butts. I was not about to contribute to the floor's deplorable condition. I checked my watch. A whole five minutes had passed. It felt more like five hours.

Eventually, the door leading out to the work area opened. Wearing a beige uniform that matched his hair, eyes, and skin, the monochromatic Morty stepped into the room. Believing he had come to tell me that the van was ready, I stood up only to sit down again when I realized Morty had come in pursuit of a cup of coffee.

Bored out of my mind, I watched as the service manager followed the printed instructions advising the use of exact change only. After taking his money, the machine rumbled in protest as it dispensed the scalding brew. This would've been fine except the needed paper cup failed to appear.

The slender, middle-aged Morty cursed as he watched the coffee disappear down the tiny drain. Not one to give up, the determined man fed the machine another batch of coins then followed up with a solid kick to its dented exterior. This time, the cup dutifully dropped in place catching what appeared to be hot cocoa.

"Well, I guess it's better than nothing," he said, sliding open the little plastic door and reaching in to retrieve the steaming beverage. "Christ, the damn cup is burning hot." Taking an oil-stained rag from his back pocket, Morty carefully wrapped it around the wafer-thin paper container.

"If I thought it'd do any good, I'd complain to the boss about this piece of crap," he said, gesturing toward the vending machine, "but with all the money problems he's got, I'm not going to bother him about losing a couple of lousy quarters, or getting the wrong thing."

The news that Cord Stanford was having money problems came as a surprise to me, although the condition of the lounge should have been a clue. I'd assumed that the room's sorry state was an oversight on management's part.

"Really? I would think that the oil franchise brings in extra business, including potential car buyers. It seems to me that Cord has come up with a win-win idea."

Morty sadly shook his head. "I don't

know. He keeps trying but, but I don't know," he repeated. "When the bottom fell out of the luxury car market, he started looking around for something to bridge the gap until business picked up again. First there was car leasing, then it was car rentals. Neither one worked out. Cord lost money on both. The worst one was the automatic car and truck wash. He sold a bunch of stock to cover that one. I know for a fact that when Winnie got wind of it, she threatened to leave him if he ever did something like that again."

The service manager dropped his naturally low voice even lower and gave me a conspiratorial wink. "That's when that Fowler fella entered the picture. Christ, that guy sure fooled old Cord."

With the vending machine doing a great imitation of a hot water heater ready to blow, I had to strain to catch what the gossipy Morty was saying.

"Yep, Cord thought Fowler was the man, all right," he said, taking time out for a swallow of cocoa before continuing. "That was until the guy's check bounced and his line of credit turned out to be nil. When Winnie found out, all hell broke loose. Him, Winnie, and the boss had a whopper of a fight right here one night when I was working late. I heard the whole thing. It was bad, real bad. Fowler swore he'd make good on the check. Then the bum ups and dies, and the boss is on the hook for mega bucks and Winnie is pissed, big time."

Morty took another swallow of the hot drink "She's gonna make somebody pay, you wait and see. She's a mean one, she is. I wouldn't want to cross her. No siree, I wouldn't put anything past that woman."

"Oh, I'm sure Winnie will stick by him, and they'll work something out," I said, looking at my watch. Even though I found Morty's revelations to be most interesting, I was more interested in getting out of there. I didn't want to be late for my meeting with Jolee Rodgers. It was important that I stick to the schedule.

Morty got the hint. Finishing the cocoa, he crushed the empty cup and stuffed it into the already full wastebasket. Looking around the room as if he'd just noticed the condition it was in, he began listing the many cutbacks initiated by Cord.

"Between you and me, Mrs. Hastings, I think it was a mistake to let the cleaning crew go. The daughter Luanne was supposed to take on the job, but from what I hear she's on the outs with her folks. One of my cousin's neighbors told my wife that it has something to do with that bartender fella, Mac, and the mess he's got himself in."

Afraid that even the mildest comment on my part would result in a fresh round of gossip, I shrugged my shoulders and smiled vacantly. Morty got the message. Twenty long minutes later, the van was ready, and I was finally on my way to Springvale.

CHAPTER
TWENTY-SIX

Whipping into Safe Harbor's parking lot, I spotted the same black Jag I'd seen on my previous visit. If it belonged to a staff member, I was obviously in the wrong business. I parked the van, tucked the speeding ticket I'd received only moments before into the glove box, grabbed my purse, and hopped out. I was hurrying past the expensive set of wheels when I noticed the vanity plate. It read: BOSS LDY. Jolee Rodgers's car? It seemed so out of character, yet when I considered how little I really knew about the director, maybe it wasn't.

In Safe Harbor's lobby, I stopped to catch my breath and was immediately accosted by a middle-aged female staff member whose attitude was as starchy and crisp as her blue-and-white uniform. Rabbitlike, the woman wrinkled her nose and advised me that I was ten minutes late. Did I realize that I'd kept the director waiting? she asked imperiously.

I decided the question didn't deserve an answer. "Why don't you do us both a favor and tell your boss I'm here," I said, none too pleasantly. Half expecting her to toss me out on my ear, I was surprised when she immediately complied. Seconds later, I was sitting in the director's office.

Pouring herself a cup of tea, Jolee Rodgers's smooth, white hands were as steady as her voice. "Ordinarily, I would never discuss such private matters with an outsider, but as you've aptly pointed out, the circumstances are far from ordinary." She carefully checked the lid and contents before covering the delicate, English porcelain teapot with a thickly padded cozy.

"Are you sure you don't care to join me, Jean, dear? If you prefer coffee, I can send one of my staff to fetch you a cup from the dining hall. Perhaps our new cook could make one of those frothy, coffee concoctions. She worked at the Koffee Kabin before joining our staff, or maybe you know that already."

What was going on here? Was she merely making small talk, or was she stalling for some reason or other? And what was that "Jean, dear" business about? I was baffled. When it came to the director, I had enough food for thought to feed an army.

Cradling the cup with two hands, Jolee Rodgers pursed her lips and blew lightly on the cup's contents. The granny-style reading glasses slid further down her aristocratic nose.

"Personally, I've never developed a taste for coffee," she said piously. "It's been my experience that in times of stress, there is nothing more soothing to one's jangled nerves than a cup of hot tea."

If this was one of those times, she sure fooled me. The woman appeared to be as calm as a mother superior presiding over vespers, reinforcing my belief that at some point in her life, a nunnery had figured prominently.

"Thanks but no thanks. I think I'll pass." What I wanted was a cigarette. For one crazy moment, I considered chewing the gum ball I'd confiscated from Kelly on Veterans Day. I was pretty sure the oversized sphere was somewhere in my purse. I was also pretty sure that Jolee Rodgers would not have approved, or been amused.

Because of the detailed message I'd left on her voice mail the previous day, Jolee Rodgers knew the purpose of my visit, giving her enough time to gather the information I was seeking. She had also had enough time to consider the consequences of sharing that information with me. I had been honest with her, and as I sat there digesting the information, I wondered if she had responded in kind.

The director took a sip of tea before gracefully reuniting the cup with the saucer. "I find the idea that this glorious institution has been the recipient of ill-gotten funds to be abhorrent. I'm sure you're aware that my goal is to protect Safe Harbor from becoming tabloid fodder. In certain circles, it has become politically correct to criticize the entire nursing home industry for the mistakes of a few."

I thought it best to ignore the remark, missing the opportunity to discuss the shortcomings in long-term care. I didn't need to emerge from the meeting as the victor in a debate over the issue. That the puritanical woman had allowed me access to Safe Harbor's financial records, without a court order, was coup enough for me. Besides, I was beginning to suspect that she might be trying to put her own spin on the information I'd requested, knowing that it was going to be used as evidence in the ongoing investigation.

"As you can see," she said with some reluctance, "the bill for this particular resident's care was quite in arrears when I signed on as Safe Harbor's director. Why my predecessor allowed this to happen was not my immediate concern. That the bill was paid in full shortly after I sent a letter of demand, brought closure to the issue." Folding her arms protectively over the leather-bound ledger, the director gave me a patronizing smile. The smile quickly disappeared when I reminded her of my intention to turn all the information I'd collected over to the proper authorities. Once that happened, it would be out of my control.

Jolee Rodgers closed her eyes for a moment, perhaps praying that when she opened them, I would be gone. "Well then," she said in a voice barely above a whisper, "I guess I'll have to wait and see how things play out. Samuel Beckett once said that we are all born mad and some of us stay that way. It seems all too true in this case. Now that you have the information you wanted, you've placed yourself in grave jeopardy. I hope you've taken steps to protect yourself. Failure to do so could have very deadly consequences. How dreadful for you."

Shrugging my shoulders in a gesture that belied my growing anxiety, I gave the director the same vacant smile I'd given Morty Butterworth. It was definitely time for me to leave. While I fished in my purse for the van's keys, Jolee Rodgers opened the middle drawer of her desk and removed a small blue envelope.

The size and color of the envelope reminded me of the "bread-and-butter" notes that people used to send within twenty-four hours of receiving a gift or a favor from a friend. Failure to do so was considered to be the epitome of bad manners. The bread-and-butter note, with its handwritten message, held its own for years before being usurped by the less personal, more convenient, thank-you card with its printed verse. These days, I suppose, e-mail has gradually replaced the thank-you card.

"This is for you," the director said, handing me the small envelope. "I promised Rosalie that I would personally see it reached you. I was going to mail it, but since you're here you might as well take it with you."

Had things been different that morning, I would have stopped and spent some quality time with Safe Harbor's oldest resident. Placing the unopened envelope in the pocket of my sweater, I asked Ms. Rodgers to give Rosalie my regards and to tell her that I would be back to visit with her in the near future.

The director agreed to do so, but warned

me not to disappoint the elderly woman. "People often make promises they fail to keep. Oh, it is so heartbreaking to see the faces of our residents when this happens, and it happens much too often. Then the staff has to step in and try to relieve their pain. That's when I miss Harrison the most. I never forgave him for leaving Safe Harbor the way he did. Oh well, what's done is done. I can't undo it, and I mustn't keep you any longer."

We said our goodbyes, and I returned to the van, where I used my cell phone to make some necessary calls. Once the calls were completed, I headed back to Seville. Nobody, not even a blackmailing murderer, likes to be kept waiting. As if it were a well-designed room, everything was coming together.

CHAPTER
TWENTY-SEVEN

I tried to pray, but try as I might, I couldn't concentrate. Perhaps it was the setting — Seville's cemetery. My mind jumped from the twenty-third psalm to the Pledge of Allegiance before landing with a thud on the alphabet. Needless to say, none of this was helping my nerves. To make matters worse, the headache I'd gotten rid of earlier had returned with a vengeance. I also had a growing case of indigestion. The waiting, in some respects, was worse than the uncertainty of what was to come and was making my mood almost as gloomy as my surroundings.

Gnarled fingers of dead ivy and a slimy moss covered most of the tomb's Indiana limestone exterior. The small, iron entrance door was partially hidden by a concrete archway. At the top of the archway loomed an imposing statue of Azreal, the Angel of Death, or maybe it was the evil Azazel. The thought of either entity lurking about was enough to send a painful stab down my spine.

Okay, I told myself, that's enough of that. Think about something pleasant like curling up in bed with a good book and a mountain of soft, velvety pillows.

I'd been sitting in the same position so long that my backside was in the throes of rebellion. A cold, cement bench is not the best place to sit if your day begins and ends with arthritis-strength aspirin. My extremities weren't doing all that well either. The cold, damp air was playing havoc with my aching fingers, robbing them of flexibility.

Seeking relief from the increasing pain and stiffness, I plunged my hands into the large patch pockets of my sweater coat. Instead of relief, I found something better — the blue envelope.

I tore open the envelope and removed the single sheet of note paper. It matched the envelope in color and quality. I was pleased to find that I wouldn't be needing my reading glasses, which was a good thing since I'd misplaced them again.

While the spidery penmanship was all Rosalie, the message was pure Roxy: "Thanks for the visit, toots. Sorry about the snooze. It sneaked up on me. Come and see me again, kiddo, and bring your friend. She's the cat's meow." It was signed with the initials R. B.

Maybe it was only wishful thinking, but after reading Roxy's note, I didn't feel quite so cold or alone.

I was about to take a much-needed stretch when a scraping sound and the rustle of dead leaves got my attention. Somebody had opened the crypt's heavy door and was fast approaching. The setting sun, which had broken through a layer of clouds, temporarily blinded me. I couldn't see but I could hear. There was no mistaking that voice. It was Jason Bowman.

"Oh my goodness, Mrs. Hastings, did I frighten you? I find that amusing since my written warnings apparently had no effect on you and this little rendezvous was your idea."

Quick as a cat, the man was at my side. In one swift move, he grabbed both of my wrists and with surprising strength pulled me to my feet. It was only then that I realized both of my legs had fallen asleep. Like a drunken sailor in the hands of the shore patrol, I had no choice but to stumble along with my captor.

Once inside the musty tomb, my eyes slowly adjusted to the semidarkness. The only source of light came from a nearly spent votive candle. With the door closed, there was a noticeable absence of fresh air. The place smelled of death and decay.

Even though Jason no longer had a hold on me, I wasn't in any position to make an escape. Leaning against the nearest wall, I fought against a persistent nausea and waited for my slumbering limbs to wake up to the fact that I needed them.

"Sorry to keep you waiting," said Jason in a pseudo-whisper, sounding like old man Twall, the undertaker. "I had to be sure you were alone. That Lieutenant Cusak is as bad as you. He's always sneaking around and asking questions. That's not a very polite thing to do." Jason's head lolled from side to side. The motion intensified my queasiness.

"You know, Mrs. Hastings, I almost hung up on you when you phoned this morning, but that would have been rude of me. Mother hated rudeness. She wouldn't tolerate it. She was such a genteel woman. She deserved, or should I say, she demanded to be treated with the utmost respect."

"Well, if it's not too rude of me to inquire," I asked with strained politeness, ignoring the pain that had wrapped itself around my back, "is that why you killed

Harrison? Because he failed to abide by your mother's code of conduct?"

"Of course. Disrespect cannot, must not, go unpunished. I learned that from my late father, bless his black heart. You could say he almost beat the subject to death."

Jason paused and rubbed his hand across his eyes. "What were we talking about? I seemed to have forgotten. Wait, I remember now. We were discussing why Harrison had to die. Did you know that he was rude to Mother and on more than one occasion? Can you believe it? The man was a nothing. At best, a hired man. He should have dropped to his knees and bowed his head in her presence."

Tiny bubbles of spittle had gathered in the corners of his mouth. Lizardlike, Jason flicked at them with his long, pointed tongue.

"The last straw was the day Mother offered the stupid oaf a peanut butter cookie from the dozen I'd purchased for her. She was in tears when she told me how he shoved the box in her face and ran from the room. Later, she saw him sharing his favorite drink, a Bloody Mary, with Rosalie Blumquist. It puzzled me why anyone would spend time with someone of her ilk when they could've been visiting with Mother. I asked Harrison what it was about the old hag that he found so fasinating. He said that Rosalie, as he called her, even after I'd revealed her unsavory past to the cad, was a fiesty old broad who amused him. Naturally, when I told Mother all of this, she was devastated. She died less than a week later, thanks to Harrison — who never did apologize."

"What led you to figure out that Harrison suffered from anaphylaxis? Was it the cookie incident or was it something else?" Speaking, like breathing, had become an effort for me, adding to my fear that perhaps I was having a heart attack.

"Actually, it was the project I'm currently working on for Valley Labs. I'm in the process of developing a new vaccine that will desensitize the severe reaction to peanuts. Ironic, isn't it. I was actually trying to improve life for someone who was making Mother's life so miserable. She certainly deserved better," Jason hissed, "and Harrison certainly deserved what he got."

His anger seemed to be escalating. Had it reach the breaking point? Not knowing this, or what response he expected from me, I resorted to a rambling account of my own mother's shoddy treatment while in a nonlicensed facility. "Your mother was lucky that you could afford to pay what Safe Harbor charges. From what I hear, the place is terribly expensive."

"Luck had nothing to do with it, Mrs. Hastings. Surely you were aware of that when you phoned me this morning and insisted on meeting with me. Tell me, who told you about my blackmailing Vernon Higgins? I'll bet it was that fat faggot Harmon. I should have gotten rid of him a long time ago. Mother warned me that he was trouble."

The last conversation I'd had with Harmon was beginning to make sense. His garbled admonishment, "Let the old dog rest in peace and allow the past to be past," was his way of saying that Jason's mother was an old dog whose death from natural causes should have been accepted by her son. When Harmon, always the pacificator, refused to believe that Harrison was responsible for Mrs. Bowman's death, Jason must have been furious. He apparently stormed out of the office, leaving behind the unrepentant Harrison and a frustrated Harmon. If only Harmon had been more of a plain talker. Instead, the bookseller's penchant for talking in circles made him a victim of the very man he sought to shield.

"So it was you who pushed Harmon off

the ladder. I'll bet you asked to see one of the leather-bound books, knowing that he kept them on the top shelf. You probably offered to hold the ladder. It wouldn't have taken much to cause Harmon to lose his balance. Once the deed was done, you slipped out the self-locking back door. Nobody, not even Matt, noticed you in the gathering crowd."

Jason acknowledged that I was correct. He smiled, immensely pleased with himself. In an effort to keep him talking, I asked him why he decided to blackmail Vernon Higgins.

He looked at me as though I was the one whose sanity was in doubt. "Because my money had run out, of course! Mother didn't have insurance and mine didn't cover her. While I had to struggle with mounting bills for her care, the Verna Higgins Foundation for Elderly Women picks up the tab for people like Rosalie Blumquist. Since I'm employed by Valley Labs, which is part of the Higgins corporate empire, Mother wasn't eligible. That shriveled-up prune of a director had the audacity to suggest if I didn't have the money then perhaps Mother belonged in the county home. That's when I decided to blackmail Vernon Higgins. Why not? If Verna's money can pay for members of the lowest class, then the bastard's money could pay for Mother, a member of the highest class."

Desparately playing for time, I asked if either Harmon or Harrison had a hand in the uncovering of the Higgins family's dark secret.

"Of course not. Harmon was much too nice, and Harrison was much too stupid. I was the only one smart enough to get the whole story out of the Blumquist hag and meld it with Mendel's findings. Aren't I the clever one?"

"Yes, you're very clever. What was it you said about somebody named Mendel finding something?" Thanks to my trip to the library, I already knew a fair amount about Mendel's Law, in particular, the law of dominance, and how the monk's botanic experiments led to the scientific study of genetics. I was playing dumb, hoping that Jason's ego would push him into a lengthy explanation of Mendel's genetic theories.

"You disappoint me, Mrs. Hastings. I thought you were smarter than most, which is why I agreed to this meeting. The idea of matching wits with a worthy opponent appealed to me. Instead, you've turned out to be just another stupid person."

I didn't care if Jason Bowman thought I

had the IQ of a rock, or a brain the size of a pea in a Mendel experiment, I had to keep him talking. It was my last, and only hope, of leaving the mausoleum alive.

"Now pay attention, dear lady, and I will explain Mendel's Law in the most basic of terms. That way you might be able to understand something I myself learned at a young age. Gregor Mendel was a man of science. His experiments with insects and plants proved that it's the dominance of certain inherited genes that determines the color of a person's skin, hair, and eyes."

Words were flowing from his mouth, accompanied by a steady stream of drool. Jason stopped speaking and wiped his wet chin with the back of his hand. He appeared to have lost his train of thought again.

The silence that followed was short-lived. My captor sprang back to life with a vengeance. "Two blues do not make a brown, if you know what I mean," he shouted at me. "Maybe you don't, but I do and so did my parents. We came from a land where color mattered. At least it did when we lived there."

His volatile mood swings notwithstanding, it still startled me when Jason suddenly calmed down and said, in a surprisingly pleasant voice, "Hey, Mrs. Hastings, I've got a riddle for you. I made it up myself. Would you like to give it a try?"

"No, not really," I mumbled, "I'm not good at riddles, especially clever ones." I didn't know how much more I could take. I was about to find out.

Ignoring my response, Jason continued. "Why is blackmail better than health insurance?" he asked before blurting out the answer. "Because unlike insurance, blackmail covers everything, and there's no deductible or forms to fill out." A sharp, high-pitched giggle escaped from Jason's gaping mouth along with a glob of saliva.

He'd moved so close to me that for an instant, I had the absurd idea that he was going to kiss me. That's when I saw the knotted, nylon stocking in his hands. One look was enough to increase the velocity of my churning stomach.

"Hey, whatever. You know what that means, Mrs. Hastings? It means that it doesn't make a whole lot of difference one way or the other to me. It also means I'm going to have to kill you. Are you ready, Mrs. Hastings? Are you ready to die?"

"You'll never get away with it," I said, surprised at the feebleness of my voice. "The cops have been tailing you ever since I called you this morning. Lieutenant Cusak should be here any minute now, you'll see."

If I thought the prospect of my son-in-law coming to my rescue was enough to throw Jason off-kilter, I was about to be proven wrong, almost dead wrong.

"Oh, I'll get away with it, all right, because I'm invisible. Nobody notices if I'm around or not. I can come and go anywhere I please, like going into the club's bar on the afternoon of the big party. That's when I added the crushed peanuts to Mac's special recipe. And it was special, wasn't it? I also sneaked in to Fowler's office and stole the medical kit from his desk. I'd noticed it the day Harmon and I met with him. Hiding it in the bar's trash bin tied that fool bartender to the crime. He so trusting, he reminds me of Harmon."

Jason began to rock back and forth on his heels. The motion added volumes to my nausea. I shivered as beads of perspiration trickled down my chest and back.

"Ah yes, Harmon. Foolish Harmon. Fancied himself to be a peacemaker," said Jason venomously, "when in reality, he was a placating nuisance. And speaking of nuisance, the only time I almost got caught was when JR came to collect some painting stuff from the storage room. She stood close enough to my hiding place that I could have easily reached out and strangled her."

Finding the idea of squeezing the life out of JR to be particularly funny, Jason laughed until he cried. He attempted to compose himself but his limbs, like his speech, had become spasmodic. He reminded me of a marionette whose strings had become entangled.

"JR didn't even notice me. Nobody ever does. You know, it bothered me until I learned to turn my invisibility into an advantage. It's become my tried-and-true method for getting away with blackmail and murder. After I kill you, I'll simply walk out of here, free as a bird."

In the glow of the candlelight Jason's hair and skin, so thin and fair, were translucent and gave his narrow head a skeletal appearance.

"Forget about being rescued by Seville's finest," he said. "I used my cell phone and called the station house while you were waiting for me. Rollie Stevens has everyone tied up in some silly meeting about lost kitties. Or was it lost kiddies?" His exaggerated pronunciation caused his mouth to twist grotesquely. "Like I said, Mrs. Hastings, whatever."

The nausea I'd been battling took control of my body. Unable to hold back any longer

I retched violently, pitching the contents of my stomach directly at the startled chemist.

With the remains of the previous night's Chinese dinner, along with the breakfast doughnut and New England clam chowder lunch splattered on his face and chest, Jason Bowman let loose with a string of vulgar curses as he sought to rid himself of the awful, malodorous debris.

"Stay away from me, Jason," I gurgled, virtually gagging on the words, "there's more where that came from, I can guarantee it."

"Why you bitch," he shouted, lurching forward. "I'll kill you with my bare hands. That way it'll be even more fun for me. It'll be even better than running over you with my car. This time, there will be no escaping from me."

Well, he couldn't say he wasn't warned. The second round was every bit as potent as the first. Once again, it was right on target. Jason began to scream. He was still screaming when the police, led by Matt, burst through the mausoleum's door.

"Sweet Jesus," someone called out, "what the hell stinks in here? It smells worse than the drunk tank down at the jail."

It was too late for me to answer. I'd already gone down the slippery slope to la-la land. Considering all I'd been through that day, passing out was a pleasure.

CHAPTER
TWENTY-EIGHT

"Well, look who's finally awake. Hey, welcome back to the land of the living, bag lady."

Charlie's voice was the first identifiable sound I heard when I opened my eyes. Fragments of images and snippets of conversations continued to flutter about in my head like confetti blowing in the wind. The odd mixture of sights and sounds, some familiar and some not, only added to my confused state of mind.

"Where am I?" I asked, wincing at the sound of my own voice. "What happened? How come this place smells like a hospital?"

"That's because it is, Mom." JR seemed to have appeared out of thin air. In reality, she had moved from her windowsill perch and joined her father at my bedside.

"And as to what happened, I can fill in some of the blanks for you. According to the newspaper reports, you were the major player in the police sting operation that resulted in the arrest of Jason Bowman. Thanks to you and the wire you wore, he's been charged with two counts of murder, one count of attempted murder, and blackmail. The good guys, led by the heroic Lieutenant Cusak, arrived in the nick of time. Jason Bowman ended up in jail and you ended up here. He's still there, and you're still alive, thank goodness."

"Thank goodness is right," Charlie added. "Had I known that you were going to use yourself as bait to catch a killer, I would've insisted on going with you." Deep worry lines had reconfigured his eyebrows, changing them from straight to crooked, and his mouth had taken on a noticeable droop.

"Charlie, if you had tagged along none of this probably would have happened. Then what? I would've been back to square one. Horatio's report reads like a manual on how to recognize a psychopath. While it convinced me I was on the right track, it wasn't proof that Jason had murdered anyone. And that's exactly what Matt said when he finished reading his copy of the report. He already had his hands full with what he believed were three unrelated cases: an unfortunate accident, blackmail, and murder. As he put it, I was long on theory and short on proof. I knew then, other than getting a full confession out of Jason, I'd never be able to convince Matt that the three cases were related. Wiring me for sound seemed to be the best way to go. Matt agreed to it because he thought there was a chance I was right about Jason blackmailing Vern Higgins."

"Well, Jason certainly fooled everyone, except you," said Charlie, holding a glass of water for me so I could take a much-needed drink. "Matt told me himself that if your trip out to Safe Harbor that morning turned out to be a bust, he was going to call off the whole operation. I'll bet it was the first time anyone ever paid for a resident's care with blackmail money."

Turning down Charlie's offer to relinquish the lone chair to her, JR solved the seating problem in her no-nonsense fashion. Nudging my sheet-encased legs to the side, she draped herself across the foot of the bed. The room was about the size of a broom closet, but it was private, and for that I was grateful.

"All the tests confirmed that the culprit in your case of almost-fatal food poisoning was Max's clam chowder," JR informed me. "The health department closed the diner down. Maybe this time, it won't reopen."

"You were the only one who ordered the chowder and actually ate it," Charlie said, clutching my hand in his. "Everyone else, including Rollie Stevens, sent it back to the kitchen."

My husband looked exhausted. More than likely, I didn't look all that great myself. I knew I was lucky to be alive. Tired but alive.

"What ever possessed you to go to Max's?" Charlie wanted to know. "I was sure you wouldn't set foot in the place even if you were starving. What were you doing at the diner?"

There was so much to tell, I hardly knew where to begin. "Max's was Matt's idea, not mine. He thought the diner was a safe place for me and a good location for the sting operation. He had me call Jason that morning and ask him to meet me there. I got tired of drinking coffee while I waited, so I ordered the clam chowder. Jason never showed up. Instead, he phoned the diner and asked for me. He claimed our little 'get together' slipped his mind, and he was calling me from the cemetery, where he was planting tulip bulbs on his mother's grave. It was his suggestion that I meet him in front of the Seville-Higgins mausoleum. I think he figured that by switching locales, he'd outfoxed me. Obviously, Jason thought

I would walk into his trap unprepared and unprotected."

Reliving the events of that unforgettable day was taking its toll on me. If I wasn't so stubborn, I would have admitted this to my family. Stifling another yawn, I tried to look and sound alert. "If you have any more questions, now's the time to ask," I said sleepily.

"Hey, as long as you're feeling up to it, Mom," said JR, ignoring the big yawn that had escaped from me, "I do have a couple of questions, and I'm sure Pops does, too."

"Such as?" I replied, stifling yet another yawn. I was trying to keep the sandman at bay. So far I'd been successful but my defenses were beginning to crumble.

Pushing my legs further aside, JR made more room for herself. "Such as, why weren't the Bowmans or Jason held accountable for his behavior while he was growing up? Animal abuse, stealing, and arson are signs of a seriously disturbed kid. How come he got away with doing stuff like that? Why didn't someone intervene? Or tell the authorities?"

"Well, for starters," I replied, "the family was living in South Africa, where Jason was born, raised, and educated as an Afrikaner. Mr. Bowman was a politically active, wealthy landowner with a reputation for racism and cruelty. The Bowmans belonged to the all-white ruling class, something they believed was their birthright. They were in a position to cover up their son's problems. Jason attended the best private schools and went on to study at one of South Africa's most prestigious universities."

"With clout like that, then why in the world did they ever leave South Africa?" JR's question caught me in the middle of an unexpected yawn. Charlie came to my rescue.

"I think I can answer that," said Charlie, taking the opportunity to show off his knowledge of world affairs. "It was the 1980s and the end of apartheid. People like the Bowmans either had to adjust and accept the sweeping political, social, and economic changes or leave the county. The Bowman family chose to leave."

"You're right," I said, "and there was something else that Horatio's international source stumbled across that I found to be interesting. Originally, the family's name was Ommen. The change to Bowman was due to a clerical error made when they went to New Zealand before coming here. The change in the name might have been a stumbling block had Valley Labs taken the time to do a background check on Jason. As luck would have it, his arrival in Indiana coincided with Valley's massive expansion program and he was hired on the spot."

Flopping back on the pillow, I yawned. "And the rest, as they say, is history, and don't ask me who 'they' are."

"Okay, I won't," said JR with a smile. "By the way, Matt told me some of what was caught on tape. Is it true what Jason said about two blues don't make a brown?"

"Yeah," I answered, fending off the sandman a while longer, knowing that if I fell asleep, my family would take it as a signal for them to leave. "But keep in mind it's the variety of color that makes a rainbow beautiful. That's something Mendel didn't stress and Jason was never taught."

"And don't forget," said Charlie, once again answering for me, "Jason's education was itself, a product of apartheid. Variety wasn't the spice of life, it was a crime."

Charlie squeezed my hand and smiled. "I say we forget Jason and all the bad things. Let's move on to something good, like Doc Parker saying you'll be getting out of here tomorrow. Pesty's going to be so happy to have you home, where you belong. That dog sure misses you."

"She's not the only one, Mom. You probably don't remember, but Matt and the twins have been here every day to see you. So have Uncle Denny and Aunt Mary."

"Did somebody mention my name?" A lilting voice floated into the room along with its owner, Mary Hastings England.

Attired in an elegant two-piece velvet-trimmed, black wool suit, Mary looked very chic. She has this thing about dressing a certain way for special occasions. White for baptisms, first communions, and weddings; red for birthdays, picnics, and graduations; and black for wakes and funerals. The only item missing from the familiar black funeral outfit was the matching velvet tam. I took its absence to be a sign of Mary's faith in my recovery.

JR scooted over, making room for Mary to sit down on the bed. I was beginning to feel a bit like the old woman in the shoe, but I wasn't about to complain. Better a crowded bedside than a lonely graveside, as my Irish mother would say.

"Oh, Gin, Denny and I have been so worried about you. He'd be here with me now except that Herbie's taken the day off. The poor soul needs some rest. What with all the nocturnal activity going on, he's lost an incredible amount of sleep."

Hearing this, Charlie dropped my hand

and nearly fell off the small chair. "For chrissakes, I knew it. I told Denny it was a mistake to install that damn door ourselves. We must have really screwed it up, or they wouldn't be messing around back there. You can call it nocturnal activity if you want, but I call it punks looking for trouble."

Clearly upset, Charlie was unaware that he was shouting at his twin sister. "I predicted something like this was going to happen. I hope to God that Denny talked to Matt about it. This is no joke. This is serious stuff."

Charlie's unexpected tirade came to an abrupt end with the appearance of the head nurse, the same one Mary and I had encountered the day we went in search of Stella. Unlike on that occasion, the nurse looked neither tired nor harried, but she did look angry. Very angry.

Taking a moment to survey the scene, she quickly zeroed in on my husband. "Sir," she said in a voice dripping with authority, "if you are unable to keep your voice down to an acceptable level, then I'm afraid you're going to have to leave. This is a hospital, not a gymnasium. In here, we talk. We do not yell. Have I made myself clear?"

Even Charlie knew that charm wouldn't get him out of this one. "Yes ma'm," he mumbled, "I'm sorry. I promise, it won't happen again."

Satisfied that Charlie had been sufficiently chastised, the nurse retreated from the room. The silence that followed was broken by the distant sound of crashing glass and Tiffany's plaintive wail. In all likelihood, the young student nurse's duties would no longer include making coffee for the doctors. I had underestimated the girl. She was a lot smarter than she looked.

While I entertained visions of skilled surgeons struggling with mundane things such as leaky filters, soggy grounds, and stained coffeepots, Charlie scowled at his sister, unaware that the nocturnal activity Mary had mentioned involved Herbie and the usual visitors from outer space. Some things are better left unsaid.

"Why in the world should Denny talk to Matt about Herbie taking time off? That doesn't make sense." Mary stopped talking long enough to select a chocolate from the large box of candy Charlie had set out for the hospital staff. "Honestly, Gin, the next time you want to solve a mystery, you should start with my brother's brain. Maybe you can figure out how it works because I sure can't."

Rolling her blueberry-colored eyes, Mary

daintily bit into an overfilled confection, releasing a tiny rivulet of buttery filling. The gooey glob slid undetected into the breast pocket of her wool suit. "Mmm, that's good. Mind if I have another one? They're real tasty but kind of dinky."

The look of bewilderment on Charlie's face was enough to set JR off. What began as a giggle erupted into full-blown laughter. If my tummy muscles hadn't objected, I would have joined in.

Carefully, I maneuvered my aching body to a full sitting position, something that allowed me a better view of the flowerfilled room. "From the looks of this place, I'm going to be so busy writing thank-you notes, I won't have time to solve even the simplest mystery for a long time, which means that your brother's brain will have to wait its turn."

"That's the best news I've had since Doc Parker told me you were finally out of the woods," said Charlie, acting as though I'd just made some profound statement. "Good. No more sticking that pretty nose of yours in other people's business, especially Matt's."

Having regained control of herself, JR reached for the box of candy. With a wink to Mary, she helped herself to a couple of pieces before passing the box back to her favorite aunt.

Watching my daughter, I was almost overwhelmed by a sudden desire to touch base with my own mother. In spite of what I'd told Jason about my mother's stay in a nonlicensed nursing home, my mother is in fact healthy and happy. She has enough family, friends, and funds to see her through the good times as well as the bad.

After my father passed away some ten years ago, Mom moved to a Southern California retirement community. She shares her place with Moira, a former nun and one of my mother's many relatives. Between trips to Las Vegas and Atlantic City, the two have taken up whale watching and are active in an organization dedicated to the preservation of California's shark population. Mother insists that when her time comes, she is to be placed on her boogie board and pushed out to sea. She hasn't been specific about details such as music, flowers, and her shroud, and to be honest about it, I'm too chicken to ask.

Mary and JR continued to rob the candy box of its contents, and Charlie continued to ignore them. Instead, he focused his attention on me.

"Sweetheart, I've been meaning to talk to

you about something," he said, taking hold of my hand again. "We're living in a time of great technology. Those of us who've learned to use it are surging ahead, and those who haven't are being left behind. Do you understand what I'm saying?"

I took back my hand. "Yes, and if you keep speaking English, I don't foresee any problem. In case you haven't noticed, I'm rather proficient in that particular language." I was back to being my old, hard self. And it felt wonderful.

Tucking both of my hands safely under the covers, I crossed my fingers and made an announcement that surprised even me. "You'll be happy to know that I won't be computer illiterate much longer. Mary and I have already signed up for a course being offered by the college. The class is scheduled to begin sometime in the spring. I believe it's listed under Computers for Blockheads in Sev-Vale's latest catalog."

Seeing the look of astonishment on her aunt's face, JR reacted immediately, slam-dunking a chocolate-covered cherry directly into Mary's open mouth. Charlie never saw a thing, or if he did, he was smart enough to pretend that he didn't.

"Hey, that's terrific sweetheart," said Charlie, sounding genuinely pleased. "Now, how about signing up for a business phone line and voice mail? I think it's time to retire that old answering machine. By the way, it's been swamped with calls for Designer Jeans. Most of them are from a Mrs. Frawley. The message is always the same. Something about needing more room. I think she needs an architect or maybe a building contractor. Since you're not either one, don't even think about getting involved."

Always one to push the envelope, Charlie wasn't finished with me quite yet. "I want your word that from now on, you're going to stick with what you do best. That means no more crime solving, Jean. It's too damn dangerous."

Cupping my face in his hands, my husband kissed me tenderly and whispered, "Here's looking at you, kid."

I never could resist his charm or that classic movie line. "Okay, Charlie, you win. You've got my word on it. No more sleuthing. And that's a promise."

Maybe, maybe not. Yawning, I uncrossed my fingers and promptly fell fast asleep.

EPILOGUE

After being shuttered for almost six weeks, Sleepy Hollow was once again up and running. Tom MacNulty agreed to take on the job of club manager. He promptly hired his new wife, Luanne, to run the bar. According to the town gossips, all was forgiven between the newlyweds and the Stanfords when Mac took Harrison's place as an investor in Cord's oil franchise.

The ditzy Tammie was promoted to Sleepy Hollow's head server and Billy Birdwell, a culinary major at Sev-Vale, became Stella Robeson's chief assistant. Stella made a quick and complete recovery from the stroke, which had turned out to be a minor one. Fearing for her safety, Matt had insisted that she be sequestered in the intensive care unit for the duration of his own investigation into Harrison's death.

Vanessa stayed on as Sleepy Hollow's board president. However, with Rollie

Stevens and Herbie Waddlemeyer filling the vacancies left by Harmon and Jason, everyone figured it was only a matter of time until she resigned. And they were right. Before the New Year was in, Vanessa was out. I guess a villa on the Riviera would be hard for anyone to resist.

Vernon keeps in touch, sending me naughty French postcards every now and then. While I don't appreciate this type of correspondence, the gang at our post office does; at least that's what I've been told by Eddie, our mail carrier.

Recently, an article appeared in *The Indianapolis Star,* one of Indiana's leading newspapers. It was all about the Bowman case and the insanity defense. The piece was written by Jason's lawyer, Jerry Dobbs.

Yesterday, a Doctor Richards of the Maynard Institute for the Criminally Insane left a message on my answering machine asking me to give him a call. He says he wants Designer Jeans to redo the patients' lounge. Before I return the good doctor's call, I think I'll have Matt listen to the tape. Maybe I'm the one who's crazy, but I swear it's Jason Bowman's voice.

A BIT ABOUT ART DECO

The Art Deco movement began in Germany shortly before the start of World War I. Its popularity increased as a result of the 1925 Paris exposition. The movement influenced the architecture of many public buildings during the 1920s, '30s, and early '40s. New York's Radio City Music Hall is a prime example of Art Deco design in that it reflects the sophistication and elegance associated with futurism, modern industry, and great wealth.

With its focus on sleek lines, bold colors, and geometric shapes, Art Deco was a rejection of the heavy, ornate, layered fussiness associated with the Victorian era. Through the use of materials such as plastic, chrome, marble, ivory, crystal, silver, gold, and bronze, designers were able to incorporate Egyptian, Mayan, and African culture into various objets d'art.

Art Deco design was embraced by the motion picture industry, especially during the 1930s. In an effort to brighten the dark days of the Great Depression, Hollywood turned out a slew of smart comedies depicting silly trials and tribulations of the very rich. Along with films like the popular Thin Man series, which featured an elegant, New York City sleuth and his glamorous wife, the public was exposed to the elements of Art Deco as interpreted by gifted costume and set designers. Produced in black and white, and with innovative lighting and camera angles, the films captured the essence of Art Deco in all its sophisticated, streamlined glory.

Tips for Achieving an Art Deco Interior

1. Start with a plan of what it is that you want to achieve, taking into consideration your budget and lifestyle. Measure the space or area in question. Be sure to include archways, windows, doors, and architectural features such as a fireplace or window seat. Convert the measurements (1/4 inch = 1 foot) and transfer them to graph paper. Using plain paper, cut out shapes representative of furniture pieces. Moving the shapes about on the graph paper allows you to try different arrangements with a minimum of effort.

2. Rent films from the 1930s that showcase Art Deco design. Films such as *Dodsworth, Topper, The Philadelphia Story,* the popular Thin Man series, and many of the early Fred Astair–Ginger Rogers musicals are sometimes featured on late night or classic TV movie channels so be sure to check your TV schedule. Examples of Art Deco can also be found in publications from the 1930s. Your local library, flea markets, and yard sales are good sources for this type of material. Movie and travel posters from the 1920s, 1930s, and the early 1940s, when properly framed, make great wall art. While collectors have sent the price of originals soaring, high-quality copies can be purchased for an affordable price.

3. Clip photos from magazines that capture the color, flavor, and mood you wish to create. Visit paint stores and home centers, where color wheels and color charts are readily available.* Ask salespersons for samples of tile, fabrics, carpeting, wall coverings, etc., for your consideration.

* Most home centers offer classes in, or feature demonstrations of, various painting techniques such as rag-rolling, dragging, stippling, spatter, color washing, and faux finishing.

Pin, tack, staple, or tape selected photos, color charts, and samples to poster board. Step back and see what pleases your eye. Make changes until you are satisfied with the end result.

4. When and where possible, go the reproduction or secondhand furniture route. With a minimal amount of change, either in fabrics and/or finishes, furniture from the 1950s can be used in an Art Deco setting. Flea markets, garage sales, auctions, and your grandmother's attic are great places to find pieces that complement an Art Deco interior.

5. Art Deco calls for bold colors (or soft colors with bold trim), textured fabrics, geometric shapes, and dramatic accent pieces. Don't allow accessories to overwhelm the overall design. One exotic floral arrangement, or an animal print area rug, can make a large statement in a small space.

6. Remember, regardless of the decor, your goal is to create a welcoming space that invites usage.

ABOUT THE AUTHOR

After successfully combining marriage, motherhood, and a business career, **Peg Marberg** returned to school, graduating in 1997 from St. Mary of the Woods College, Terre Haute, Indiana. Now a full-time writer, Peg and her husband are part-time residents of Indiana and Arizona, where they enjoy the company of family, friends, and of course, the irrepressible Chaco, aka Pesty.

We hope you have enjoyed this Large Print book. Other Thorndike, Wheeler, and Chivers Press Large Print books are available at your library or directly from the publishers.

For information about current and upcoming titles, please call or write, without obligation, to:

Publisher
Thorndike Press
295 Kennedy Memorial Drive
Waterville, ME 04901
Tel. (800) 223-1244

or visit our Web site at:

www.gale.com/thorndike
www.gale.com/wheeler

OR

Chivers Large Print
published by BBC Audiobooks Ltd
St James House, The Square
Lower Bristol Road
Bath BA2 3SB
England
Tel. +44(0) 800 136919
email: bbcaudiobooks@bbc.co.uk
www.bbcaudiobooks.co.uk

All our Large Print titles are designed for easy reading, and all our books are made to last.